# Jude, the Creature and the Book of Truth

## By Gary Lewis-Baztán

ISBN: 978-1-7391440-3-6

Olcan Press

First published by Olcan Press on 15<sup>th</sup> April 2023

Olcan Print/Press are a subsidiary of the Olcan Group

6 Park Hill, Ealing
London, W5 2JN, UK
Email: team@olcan.co
www.olcan.co

Content copyright © Gary Lewis-Baztán

For permission contact:
team@olcan.co

A CIP record of this publication is available from the British Library.

First printed March 2023
Paperback ISBN: 978-1-7391440-3-6

| **Chapter Title** | **Page Number** |
|---|---|

# CHAPTER ONE
## JUDE

He'd been in quite a state when he'd first rushed back into the office. His clothes were completely wet through and he'd needed a hot tea to steady his shakes. But after Jude had typed the last words, 'Jude Holmes', he smiled broadly. Another article that he'd written would be published in the Daily Gazette and this would be his first proper crime story. Although his work was published almost every day, he still found there was no better feeling than knowing what he'd written would be read by others. He walked the short distance to the print room and then left the office. He jumped in his car and headed for home a satisfied man. It was a late Thursday night. He still had to pick up Dylan from his mum's house and most likely get an earful from her; then he had to get home, make himself some dinner (it was most likely a microwave meal, a just-about-edible meal), and put his head down and get some rest. He had to be back in the office fairly early the following morning.

The *Daily Gazette*, Friday, 26th October 2018

**YOUNG BOY ATTACKED LOCALLY – HAS WAR HERO LOST**

**HIS MORALS?**

Harold Larkin is known to his local community and neighbours as a gentleman who has served his country and did them proud. When his country called, Harold served with distinction. In the face of danger, he didn't bat an eyelid. But yesterday evening a witness claimed he saw Mr. Larkin batter a 16-year-old boy into a coma.

Harold was 16 himself when he was called up to go to war in 1943. Now 91 years old, you would think Harold would have learnt from his past experiences – apparently not.

Jay Whittle was with his friend playing football on a field at the back of Harold's house in Newton Mead's Park View area. After Jay had kicked the ball into Mr. Larkin's back garden, he jumped the fence to collect his ball. He was met with a baseball bat to his head.

The Daily Gazette spoke to one of Jay's friends for his account of what happened. Lewis Darlington was understandably very shaken, but he told the Gazette: "When Jay jumped over the fence, I heard old Harold Larkin shouting obscenities – this was quickly followed by a sickening thud."

Jay is in a serious condition, in a medically induced coma. Mr. Larkin was arrested shortly after the incident but released without charge only a few hours later.

Jude Holmes

On Friday morning police spokesman Sergeant Wilkins released the following statement:

As a strong, close-knit community, we are all shocked by what seems to all a truly terrifying incident. We are all concerned about Jay's condition and we have trained officers helping his family through this. We have started an investigation into what happened, but as I'm sure you can understand, I will currently not be able to give any further information on the case. But what I will say to all our residents is this is a safe place to live, with one of the lowest rates of crime in the UK. Rest assured the person who committed this abhorrent attack won't go unpunished, but I can you tell you with full confidence this is a one-off incident. But to allay some of your concerns, over the next few weeks you'll see a stronger police presence on our streets and we will continue to put your safety first – your safety is, of course, paramount to us. Thank you for your time.

Jude kicked off his duvet. He stretched his arms as wide as they could go and yawned. He had never had the need to set an alarm clock. Barring last night, he tried to go to bed every night at 10pm and would naturally wake up at 6am. Today was a Friday morning and he wasn't expected at work until 8.30am, especially as he'd not long left work. He would follow his routine no matter if it was a workday or not.

Slowly, Dylan crawled out of his bed and yawned; he looked like he was imitating Jude.

'Are you hungry, boy?' Jude asked.

Dylan ran over to Jude excitedly. He jumped with his two front paws almost pushing Jude over as they landed on his chest.

'Come on then, boy – let's go downstairs,' Jude cheerfully instructed.

Jude filled both Dylan's stainless-steel bowls to the brim,

one with fresh cold water and the other with a dry dog food. He left Dylan to devour his food and make a mess with the water. Jude ran upstairs and changed into his gym gear. He wasn't going to the gym but he had two dumb-bells at home and also liked to use his own weights to exercise. He did 100 sit-ups and 200 press-ups every morning – without fail. Forty-five minutes later and it was time to take Dylan for a short, fifteen-minute walk to drop him off at Dog Central (the local dog-sitters) – and then a slightly quicker walk back home for Jude. This gave him twenty minutes to get ready for work and leave his house. This was something he had down to a fine art.

He paced it to his desk, holding a double macchiato, a ham, cheese and mustard panini, and an on-the-green-side banana. His usual breakfast, except the banana was usually a little bit more yellow. He flicked his laptop on and looked around. For a Friday the atmosphere was odd, not so jolly. He had noticed not even happy Allan had smiled when he'd come in. Allan was two weeks away from his retirement and seemed to be always in a joyous mood.

'Jude – Mr Tomkins said when I see you to say, office now,' Bella said, in a no-nonsense tone.

'Strange – did he say it like that?' Jude asked, as he got up and started walking over to Mr Tomkins' office, shaking his head and not waiting for Bella's reply. Bella was a new team member; she started in August. She was also a writer like Jude; she wrote a comedy section for the paper, called Fun Times. She mocked local politicians and anyone she disliked it seemed. Jude hadn't taken to her. He hadn't seen her smile once, and it was her job to make readers laugh. He hadn't read any of her work and had no intention of reading any of it either. He could hear her mumble 'He did actually' as he walked away.

He knocked lightly on Mr Tomkins' door and waited

patiently for the go-ahead to open it and go inside.

'Yes, come in, Jude,' Mr Tomkins said loudly and in a sharp tone.

'Bella said …'

'Yes, I wanted to talk to you about your article that we published for this morning's paper.'

'Okay, sure.'

'Not okay – take a seat,' Mr Tomkins said. 'I'm afraid the paper only went out this morning and we've already received numerous complaints,' he continued. 'Mr Larkin is a war hero and, more importantly, a man who after the Second World War worked in a highly important role for the government.'

'He hit a boy in the head with a baseball bat, did he not?' Jude asked. 'Did I not tell the truth?'

'Do you work for the police or as a journalist?' Mr Tomkins asked.

'A journalist,' Jude replied.

'You didn't witness the incident yourself and you wrote a one-sided story and one with a title that insinuated Mr Larkin had not only put a boy in a coma, but he was a man who had lost his marbles,' Mr Tomkins said. 'I've been told by our legal eagle that if we don't terminate your contract then we can expect a lawsuit. And even with you gone we'd still likely face plenty of grief for what got printed. What on earth were you thinking? This could bankrupt us. We are a local paper; we can't …'

There was a pause in the conversation. Jude shuffled around in his seat; he knew there was only going to be one outcome here.

For a moment he considered responding forcefully by suggesting he could in turn sue the Gazette for wrongful dismissal if he was fired, but thought better of it.

'Harold Larkin is a pillar of the local community. The

Gazette, needs to apologise in print to him quickly and head off any further unpleasantness,' continued Mr Tomkins. 'What I would advise, and I urge you to take note of this, is right now, you walk out of my office with your head held high and you go back to your desk and immediately type up your resignation, right now.' He put his head down to look at his laptop and waved his hand to gesture to Jude to leave the office.

Jude got up out of his seat and opened the door to Mr Tomkins' office. He was shaking his head and said quietly but loud enough for Mr Tomkins to hear, 'Right now, right now – idiot.' And he slammed the door behind him.

He knew Mr Tomkins was right: if he didn't resign then his CV was screwed. He didn't have the money to take the Gazette to court and by the sounds of things, Mr Larkin would probably know the bloody judge, or worse still, Mr Larkin would be the judge the way his luck was going.

He typed up a short resignation and gave it to Bella to hand in to Mr Tomkins, not letting her know what it was. But he had a feeling everyone in the office knew what was happening. He took a leaf out of Bella's book and made for the exit without smiling at anyone, not even happy Allan.

# CHAPTER TWO
## JUDE

He pressed his foot slightly too hard on the accelerator. He needed to get as far away from work, and as fast, as possible. He opened the window in his car to let the cold, morning, fresh-air breeze hit his face. He knew he had some important decisions to make. He gradually eased his foot off the gas, and started to mentally write a list of notes in his head, whilst he drove back to his house. The last time he would make this journey. The thought that kept reoccurring was, if it wasn't for Mr bloody Tomkins, he wouldn't have been working for the Gazette in the first place. Just over a year ago, he was headhunted from the online magazine *Man Issues*, which he used to write for. He knew if he asked Nigel, *Man Issues* would take him back, but he'd helped Nigel start up the business and saw going back to it as a step backwards in his career. When working for *Man Issues*, he was a writer who was writing about trivial inconveniences to men's lives that were humorous, but for the Gazette he'd turned into a journalist, who reported on what was happening in the area he lived in – what he reported mattered.

Since Jude had received a hefty inheritance a few years

ago, when his Great Auntie Lou had died, money was not his priority. In that respect, he knew he was lucky – well, as lucky as a man could be who had just got sacked for doing what he was hired to do – reporting the news.

He arrived back at home and was horrified when he saw his front door had been sprayed with a red Nazi swastika. He fumbled in his trouser pockets for his house keys. As he found them, he heard a car rev its engine loudly a couple of times nearby. He found his house key, put it in the lock, turned it quickly and then pushed the door open. The car now sounded a lot closer. He turned to see a blue car driving into his garden and not too far away from him. He stood still; he was frozen. The car screeched its wheels fast and braked hard before it almost hit Jude and drove straight into his house. The car then swivelled around and sped off without stopping. He only thought afterwards, he should have taken note of the registration plate. He was shocked. He looked around and couldn't see any witnesses. Maybe the driver was new or old and they put their foot on the gas by mistake, he thought. He was still standing in the doorway when he heard his house phone had started to ring.

'I can't believe you would write such …'

'Mum, I'm really not in the mood for your usual criticism of my work,' Jude said abruptly, his voice notably shaken. Jude's mum, Mary, was an author herself and would often call her son to give him some constructive feedback, which is what she called it. But Jude was sure feedback was meant to be mixed with negative and positive remarks. Her feedback was almost always only negative.

'Anyway, how did you know I was at home?' Jude asked.

'Oh, are you letting me speak now? You're the talk of the town, dear. Everyone knows about the article – I'll be villainized for years to come,' Jude's mum said.

'Make it all about you why don't you, like usual,' Jude said.

'You know I've had to quit my job. My name is tarnished in this industry – forever.'

'Yes, well I thought you had been sacked to be honest. You can't go around making stuff up. Poor Harold. I mean, really.'

'Poor Harold? Yes, poor Harold. Silly me for reporting the truth.'

'Truth? I'm not sure about that, son. The police have just arrested a 16-year-old with attempted murder.'

Jude's heart skipped a beat and he dropped his phone.

# CHAPTER THREE
# JUDE

A darkness, a feeling of shame, hit Jude like Thor's hammer on impact. After hanging up the phone to his mum, he walked straight over to his oak veneer spirits cabinet and grabbed a bottle of 12-year-old single malt; he'd been saving the whisky for a special occasion. This was not a special occasion, but Jude believed he needed a drink; he deserved a drink – a strong one. He sat at his solid pine writing desk and swirled the golden liquid around in a crystal glass, one his dad had once used. Jude had kept it as a keepsake when he was a child, to remember his dad when he wasn't there. His dad was still alive, but growing up he was hardly ever there. He'd never noticed his glass had gone missing and he'd never said anything.

Jude remembered his notes that he'd written about Harold and they were kept in the bottom left-hand draw of the desk, closest to the floor. That evening, he looked through them; a few points stuck out like a sore thumb. Lewis was pale and he'd smelt of sick, but mainly the 'no eye contact' stood out. Jude looked up from his notes; he knew what he saw.

He stopped what he was doing. He had forgotten about the time; the day had flown by. He looked at his phone in a panic. He'd received five missed calls from Dog Central and two voicemails.

'Damn!' Jude shouted. He was annoyed; he'd only just remembered Dylan. He felt guilty; Dylan would miss him. He'd be charged an extra £20 for lateness – he was supposed to pick him up at 5.30 and was already two hours late. He contemplated calling a taxi, but Dog Central was only a five-minute drive. He grabbed his car keys and headed for the door.

He realised he'd made a mistake two minutes into the drive, but he was halfway there; there was little point in turning back. He arrived at Dog Central and managed to park okay, without bumping into any other car, person or inanimate object – that was good parking in Jude's eyes right now. He swung his driver's car door open and the air immediately extenuated his intoxication; he did his best to walk in a straight line to the front door. The door opened before he made it; Dylan bounded over. Jude made his apologies as quickly as he could and promised to pay the extra charge by the end of the week. As he got back into his car, he was sure he'd got away with his drunkenness.

On the drive home, he was becoming paranoid. He had been fired/had quit work, had a Nazi sticker sprayed on his door, had nearly been run down by some lunatic and his mum had given him her usual feedback before telling him his report was factually incorrect and that someone else had been arrested – not Harold. This was all in one day. Now he was drink-driving, something he'd never done before and, on the whole, he deplored. He was losing respect for himself; maybe Mr Tomkins and his mum were right to criticise him.

Two cars behind he could see a police car. He slowed and was going 5mph slower than the speed limit of 50mph. He then thought this made him look more guilty, so he sped up and was now going slightly above the speed limit at 52mph. As he sped up, the red Renault behind also sped up and went to overtake him, going into the right-hand lane. But now Jude was going too fast. He didn't know if he should slow down for the impatient Renault driver to overtake or if this would risk him looking suspiciously slow again. He slowed down. The police car flashed its lights and the sirens went on. Jude slowly started to pull over.

'A perfect end to such a perfect day,' he sarcastically muttered to himself, hitting his leg simultaneously with his fist. 'I'm sorry, Dylan – looks like you'll have to put up with my mum again.'

The police car sped past Jude's car and after the Renault that was now easily going at 80mph, and they weren't stopping; it was a full-on chase.

Jude wiped his brow, relieved he wasn't going to be arrested but a little disappointed he wouldn't be able to write about the police pursuit of the Renault. As he took the junction off the motorway, he saw the same blue car again as earlier – he was sure of it. It continued on the motorway.

Dylan had made it to the front door before him. Jude felt for his house keys, momentarily thinking he'd lost them. Dylan snatched a large envelope off the floor, holding it between his teeth, and he ran off before Jude could reach for the post.

'Dylan, come back, boy!' Jude shouted, in what only a dog owner could recognise as a stern but friendly dog-owner voice. Dylan didn't listen as he shook his head from side to side trying to open the post. Jude was a bit mystified; he hadn't noticed the post earlier today, but his head had been all over the place.

'Come on, Dylan – bring it here, boy, and I'll give you a treat,' Jude said. He walked to get a dog treat out of the cupboard, one especially designated for dog food in the kitchen. A sudden yelp made him turn around and run back to the hallway.

As he made it to Dylan, he could see he was lying down, collapsed on the floor. 'What is it, boy?' Jude asked. He looked down at Dylan, who was crying and starting to shake, and was confused.

'What the hell?' Jude jumped backwards. Slithering out from underneath the envelope was an almost completely black snake.

# CHAPTER FOUR
# JUDE

To say he was tired, which would be an understatement. Jude was beyond exhausted – he'd spent half of last night at Oakwell Veterinary. Lucky for Jude, and especially for Dylan, after a few moments of panic, a lovely overnight emergency veterinarian named Kyle was on hand when they arrived. The veterinary had a closed sign on the front door when Jude frantically knocked on its doors and windows, shouting for help, hoping somebody was there. Shortly afterwards, Kyle calmly opened the doors. Jude explained to Kyle that he thought it was an adder, as he had recently written a story about UK snakes, the adder being one of two native ones. And this snake had a large head like an adder.

Jude had remembered he should carry Dylan if bitten as well and he didn't want to put him down – he didn't want to hand him over to Kyle. He was hoping his small amount of knowledge would help. He appreciated the calm way Kyle welcomed him in and how he explained he had given Dylan a small anti-venom injection and would monitor him through the night; but he was fairly sure there was nothing to be overly concerned about and shortly after 12pm, he advised Jude to go home and get some sleep. He said he'd call him in the morning to update him on Dylan's condition and all things being well, he'd let him know when he could come and collect him.

Jude arrived back home in the early hours of the morning. The house was cold and it felt empty. He was used to his own company, without the companionship of another human to share, to find comfort in, to offload after a difficult day, but normally he had Dylan. Without him, he felt alone. He walked into the kitchen and opened the fridge looking for a snack. It was almost bare, bar a microwave meal; he was due a weekly shop. His stomach rumbled but he didn't feel hungry – he felt sick. He was exhausted, restless and deflated. He walked into the living room, collapsed on the sofa and cried and cried, until after around half an hour, he had no tears left; he could cry no more and fell into a deep sleep.

The phone started to ring. Jude jumped bolt upright off the sofa – he'd been solidly asleep for around six hours. He answered. It was Kyle, the vet, to say Dylan was okay and he could come and collect him when ready. He was relieved and thought of having a quick shower before jumping in the car to collect him. He headed upstairs but ran straight back down when his phone started to ring again.

He answered. 'Who has been a naughty boy?' a robotic voice said. Jude laughed and contemplated hanging the phone up straight away, but he was intrigued.

'Who is this?' Jude asked.

'This is not your problem; I'm someone you do not want to know,' the voice said.

'Okay, are you having a laugh?'

'No. I'll give you some advice: you need to move house!'

'Have you been following me?' Jude asked.

There was a sudden smash. A brick flew through the front

window, smashing the glass in its path. Jude ducked, dropping his phone and putting his hands over his head, a reaction to protect himself. Although the brick landed nowhere near him, he was shaken; his hands trembled. He slowly approached the front door and looked outside, but he couldn't see anyone. He went back to the living room and picked up the phone – he expected the pranker to have hung up.

'Robot man, you still there?' Jude asked.

'Pack your things, now,' the robotic voice demanded, and the line went dead.

# CHAPTER FIVE
## JUDE

'Another Doom Bar please, mate,' Jude said to the barman.

'Make that two, mate,' Ryan said.

Jude hadn't noticed when Ryan came into the pub. He'd arranged to meet him at 2pm, but had arrived half an hour early and had already sunk two pints whilst waiting for his friend.

'No problem, lad,' said the scruffy, young-looking barman.

They sat in a quiet corner of the pub, a drinking haunt from the past. The Sunken Ship was the pub Jude used to meet up with Ryan in when they were teenagers and not old enough to be drinking. In the more recent past, they used to meet every Saturday to watch the football. Work had taken over – life had taken over.

'Hey, mate – this is like the good old days,' Ryan said. 'We should make this an all-day session. What d'you reckon?'

'I suppose so,' Jude replied. He'd wanted to meet his old pal for drinks but wasn't really in the mood to chat. He thought it looked better to be drinking with someone than sitting in the pub and getting wasted on his own.

'You could sound a little more enthusiastic,' Ryan said. 'We haven't met up for drinks in – I can't even remember how long.'

'Alright, calm down – I was thinking, that's all,' Jude said. 'Of course, I'm chuffed to meet up. We're going to make this one to remember – I can tell.'

Earlier in the day, after Jude had received the robotic call, he had decided against calling the police. He quickly grabbed his fancy, silver, aluminium suitcase and filled it with what he would call his essentials. He then put his case in the boot of his car.

After packing, he drove to Oakwell Veterinary surgery and picked up Dylan. He then put his foot on the gas and headed to his local DIY store, Units. Dylan sat in the front passenger seat next to him. Jude wanted some wood to repair his newly broken window. He was swiftly in and out of Units and then sped back home. He blocked the window up as best he could and then walked next door to his neighbour's house and organised with him, an old chap called Gary, to come around for the setup of his new CCTV and window replacement. Jude had asked when buying the wood in Units about the window repairs and they kindly helped him organise it all, even the CCTV. He gave Gary a spare set of keys, and then called Ryan to arrange the drinks.

Jude was six Doom Bars in and was drunk.

He had decided not to tell Ryan too much about the day he'd had, although he could tell Ryan looked slightly perplexed that Dylan was out with them. Ryan never asked and the pub owner didn't seem to mind about his dog being in the pub. He wanted this to be a day to enjoy, although the same thoughts kept running through his mind. Should he have called the police? But what good would that have done? The police had let a man free who had attempted to murder a teenager. Jude did have a catalogue of reasons to call the police: the Nazi sticker, the snake, the brick through the window and the threatening robot call demanding he left his house. Plus the blue car that nearly ran him down and the fact he was sure he was being followed.

# CHAPTER SIX
## JUDE

The thought of last night and the number of beers Jude had sunk had brought back an array of memories, mostly a feeling of hurt from the past. The Sunken Ship was Jude and Ryan's pub to drink in; it always had been. Jude could remember many good times over the years, especially when they were too young to be drinking – that was half the fun. The adrenaline of 'will we or won't we get served' was the best part. He was certain the bartenders knew they were only 16 but in those days it didn't matter; they had money and the bartenders wanted their money. They wanted to get pissed and they had the beer; it was win-win for all. These days it was different: life had changed and Jude sometimes thought not much had changed for the better. The bad feelings threatened to overtake him but he was determined to keep them at bay. He could remember why he wanted so desperately to be out of the house and to be with Ryan and his other pals at the time and to be drinking at the pub – he always needed to forget. Jude shook his head; he needed to move. He needed purpose; but mainly, he needed a change of scenery.

He had slept most of the day in his car, and it smelt foul, even with the windows open. The day had passed him by without him doing much. He'd eaten a Cornish pasty and drank a hot coffee that he'd walked to a local patisserie. He had needed the fresh air. He'd also managed to drink a whole litre bottle of flat lemonade he'd left in his car weeks ago. But the main thing he'd done was get over his hangover, the cold sweats and the feeling of sickness. He walked around the town centre aimlessly with Dylan and then they walked back to the car. He found his toothpaste and toothbrush from the boot and settled in for another night in the car with the dog.

A persistent buzzing sound was going off in the car. Jude rubbed his eyes as the morning light shone in through the car windows. His phone was ringing but he couldn't find it. He rustled about looking for it. He eventually got out of his car and realised it was in his back pocket. He looked at his phone; missed call Dad, it read. He rubbed his eyes again and pressed redial.

'Hi, son. How are you doing?' his dad said.

'I'm feeling sharp,' Jude said in a croaky, sarcastic voice.

'You don't sound it,' his dad said. 'You sound rough, like I've just woken you up.' Jude looked at his watch; it was only 7am.

'It is pretty early. I think you'd find most people will be sound asleep or half asleep at 7 in the morning,' Jude said. 'Anyway, what is it? Have you been talking to Mum?'

'As it happens, she did phone me,' his dad said. 'And you know she doesn't phone me much. Actually, scrap that – she doesn't phone me. So I knew it must be important.'

Jude supressed a laugh. He would have laughed if this was a normal family. But there's a bloody good reason she doesn't phone you, he thought.

'Anyway, she did phone me and she was concerned about

you,' his dad said. 'She said you've lost your job. Is that true, boy?'

'Do you know what? She's a gossip, an old gossip. Me losing my job is none of your concern and it's not Mum's either,' Jude said in a monotone voice, supressing the anger rising up inside him. He didn't want his dad to gain anything from this conversation. 'I shouldn't have answered your call. I have to go now.'

He ended the call and threw his phone on to the passenger seat. He breathed in a deep breath and released slowly. He shook his head, got back in his car and put the key in the ignition.

He drove at his own pace. He was going somewhere he wanted to go to – it felt right. He thought about calling his mum. How dare she speak to his dad, but he knew she'd turn it around and it would be his fault. He dreaded her judgement, her criticism, and could do without it. He called her anyway. Luckily, it went straight to voicemail: 'Hi, Mum. I've decided to go on holiday for a few weeks – keep my head low for a while, you know. I have a lovely little cottage booked in the Cotswolds. Call me if you need me. Take care. Love …' It beeped before he had finished his message.

He hadn't booked a room to stay at in a hotel or bed and breakfast; he hadn't booked a place to stay full stop. He liked the thought of turning up somewhere unannounced; the not knowing was a little bit exciting and he wasn't going to the Cotswolds.

# CHAPTER SEVEN
# JUDE

Jude had driven until he was too tired to continue. He had an idea of the kind of location and place he wanted to stay in; he headed south. He thought about waking up and seeing the crisp blue skies and yellow beach as the sun rose in the morning. He liked the thought of hearing the crashing waves as he took a bare-footed stroll in the sand first thing in the morning, only seeing maybe one or two other people walking their dogs. Dylan would love that, and he would love it too, he thought. All those different scents and textures would be dog heaven and waking up and going straight to the beach was idyllic for Jude as well. He looked up and saw a sign: Bournemouth. Somewhere in Bournemouth. He wanted to be near the coast – this was ideal.

He'd been driving for most of the day. He'd stopped for walks with Dylan, taking his time as there was no need to rush; he had no work and no responsibility except for Dylan. Why had he always been in such a rush? Everyone is in a rush – why? Especially as he didn't desperately need the money, why had he bothered trying to be like everyone else? He had no wife or children to provide for, his mum was tough as old boots and his dad, well, his dad didn't matter; he could take of himself – he always had. He would do this more often, he promised, after all this drama at home was over. He'd look out for number one more often than not, and Dylan of course.

He drove on the roads closest to the sea, but it was getting dark and he was too tired to drive much longer; he needed to stop. He could see the beach and thought about the long morning walks with Dylan. He hoped they would allow dogs on the sand. 'Little Bournemouth Hotel,' he saw on a crooked sign outside a pub. He thought, they'll probably have rooms, surely. He hoped. They had free parking spots, so that was a bonus.

He walked into the hotel/pub and chatted to the owner – an old lady whose skin looked like it could do with a couple of thick coats of moisturiser. If that was what the sea and sun did, he was having second thoughts about this new lifestyle already. She had a room going spare, luckily. They were normally fully booked; she repeated how fortunate he was to get a room. If she hadn't have had any rooms available, he'd envisaged another cramped night with Dylan sleeping in his car again.

'It is 100 pound for the night, but you're lucky as I'll throw you in a free pint as well, because you're handsome – you could be a Bond you know,' the old landlady said, winking. She smiled and revealed teeth more crooked than the sign that stood outside her pub. She started to pour the drink, but she suddenly realised he had a dog – he had Dylan sat with him.

'You're not taking that dog up to your room, are you?' she asked.

'Where am I meant to put him?' he said. 'I can't leave him in my car all night alone, alright.' He got up from his seat. 'I'll have to look for somewhere else.'

'You'll be lucky, Mr Bond, at this time. An extra tenner and you can stay the night,' she said, and winked at him.

Jude laughed. 'Okay, go on then. Like you said, I have little choice,' he said. He knew earlier she didn't really want to give him a free pint. She was a crook. She'd done that before; he would put a wager on it. He sat back down and settled back in, sipping at his 10-pound pint.

He finished his pint of Doom Bar and followed it up with a couple more pints and a few packets of salt and vinegar crisps. He was starving; he remembered he hadn't had a real meal all day. But the pub wasn't serving cooked food – it was too late. He was hungry but he didn't fancy going out and looking around for a takeaway restaurant. He was shattered so he called it a night.

# CHAPTER EIGHT
## JUDE

Once Jude had made his way up to his room, brushed his teeth and got ready for bed, he felt re-energised. He looked at Dylan, who had already fallen asleep on the end of his bed.

'Night, boy. We'll go on another adventure tomorrow,' he said, and ruffled Dylan's long scruffy hair on the top of his head. Dylan opened one eye, but he soon fell back to sleep.

Jude hadn't been able to go through his normal exercises so he decided it was a good time now to do some press-ups and sit-ups. Afterwards, the endorphins that pumped around his body made him feel even more alert. He played with his phone. He was bored and knew he must be tired; he must need some sleep. He made an effort to not look at his phone anymore. He turned the lights off, drew the curtains and tried his best to get some sleep. Eventually, he started to drift off.

The fear – he remembered the intensity; he felt the pure panic.

It was the middle of the night. He woke up in a cold sweat, his sheets saturated with his sweat. He was still half asleep as he rummaged about looking around the room, until he found the remote to put the television on. The lights hurt his eyes so he closed them, but he needed the sound of the TV to relax him. He waited a couple of seconds and opened his eyes again, but he couldn't get back to sleep. He walked over to the sink, turned the tap on to cold and sipped at the water. He walked back over to his bed and sat upright against the headboard with the pillows behind his back. He stared at the screen, not watching, not listening, but half asleep, his eyes still open.

Slowly, he drifted back off to sleep with his eyes still half open. His usual nightmare haunted his dreams. Talking to himself, he repeated the words, 'the blood, so much blood'.

# CHAPTER NINE
## JUDE

The light from outside was shining through a gap in the light nylon curtains and it woke Jude up. He hadn't heard the footsteps that were fast approaching his room. Last night, he ended up completely falling asleep with the TV still on.

'Wakey-wakey, boy,' he said.

Dylan was already stretching and doing some big open-jaw yawns.

Jude stretched and yawned himself, this time mimicking his dog. He walked over to the curtains and opened them fully. The news was playing in the background; he could hardly hear it, so he picked the remote up and was about to turn the sound up. He jumped as there was someone banging on the door. Realising he was standing in a pair of boxer shorts only (he'd been wearing the same boxer shorts for a few days), he quickly looked around the room for his clothes. He pulled up his trusted blue jeans over his old boxers and put on a creased, white, V-neck T-shirt. He walked over to open the door to his room, but abruptly stopped. What if someone had followed him? What if the blue car, the car that had sped on to his garden and towards him at his house, the car he'd seen again on the motorway, what if they had been sent out to get him? To hurt or kill him? His imagination was going into overload. He looked around the room for something heavy, just in case he needed to protect himself. He picked up a bottle of his favourite fragrance; that would do some damage. He was ready – he had a weapon.

'Are you still alive in there?' a lady asked.

The landlady with the crooked teeth. Thank God, Jude thought. 'Yes, I'm well, thank you,' he said, feeling relieved. He really didn't fancy his chances if he had to fight someone; he had never won a fight in his life, not one.

'Do you want a full English breakfast in bed or are you coming down?' She asked in a croaky, smoker's voice.

'I'll come down. This is a very good service – is this all included?' Jude asked knowingly. He was winding her up.

'Of course not. It's £9.99 for breakfast with a coffee or a cup of tea and an extra £2 for a fresh orange as well. I'll see you downstairs,' she said. 'Oh yes, will it be coffee or tea and would you like a fresh orange as well? Before I go.'

'Coffee and a fresh orange as well, thanks,' Jude said. He laughed to himself and put the fragrance back down, but not without spraying a couple of squirts under his chin first. He grabbed his phone and his wallet and headed downstairs. If he thought he was hungry last night, he was starving now, and although he had brought food for Dylan, he was sure he'd be happy with a few sausages as well.

Straight after eating, he headed back upstairs to his room and made the most of the showering facilities – it was well needed. He felt a new man afterwards. He then packed the few bits he had and headed back down to the bar and made sure everything was paid; he didn't want the landlady running after him. With everything ready, he and Dylan got back on the road.

# CHAPTER TEN
# HAROLD
# TEN DAYS BEFORE

He'd spent most of the day thinking about the past; all of the memories he'd shared with her, with his wife, these were just his and his alone these days. There isn't much you take with you when you're gone, he thought; you don't even get to keep your memories. Harold tenderly touched the glass of the framed photo of their wedding day, breathed in deeply, took a step backwards and then smiled. 'My sweet Barb,' he said, as he walked over to the stairs.

He jumped and stepped backwards. There was a loud crash as a ball struck the window in the kitchen.

'Pesky kids again – every damn day,' he muttered, before he climbed the staircase and walked into his bedroom. He opened the window and shouted, 'Come and get your ball – I dare you!'

Jay stuck his finger up at him and ran and jumped the fence into Harold's garden. He grabbed his ball, turned to face Harold and stuck his finger up again, before he jumped back over the fence.

'Lewis, I would expect better from you!' Harold shouted, before closing the window firmly.

Harold had known Lewis since he was a baby; he'd known his mum when she was a baby also. He'd known Lewis' mum very well; he felt as though she was like the daughter he'd never had. Lewis was the grandchild he never had. In fact, he had bought the ball as a present for Lewis, the ball that kept hitting his house. It was just a few weeks ago that Jane, Lewis' mum, had confided in Harold. She said Lewis was hanging out with the wrong crowd and getting into trouble. Harold had thought a football would be a good distraction. How much trouble can you get into with a football? he had thought. He didn't realise at the time Lewis and his friend would be playing football so close to his house.

Later, in the evening, Harold locked the back door in the kitchen and then the front door. He double-checked them again before heading up to bed that night. He was used to being on his own now. He'd been on his own for a long time, but the loneliness and paranoia once it was dark outside never got any easier. He headed upstairs and after a quick wash of his face and teeth, he was nestled up under his warm duvet. The same old red and white flowered duvet he had shared with his late wife.

# CHAPTER ELEVEN
# HAROLD
# NINE DAYS BEFORE

Harold woke up in a bad mood. He'd hardly slept and the little sleep he'd managed had given him a sore neck; he could hardly move it. He opened his curtains that overlooked the field, cursed and headed into the bathroom. He took a painful staggered piss, gargled with some mint mouthwash and then brushed his teeth. He looked in the mirror and an old face stared back at him; his old face was staring back at him.

He thought about his wife, how he'd once told her, 'I don't think I'll ever age, Barb. I'm too good-looking to get old.' Barbara had laughed.

'Really? Is that so. Who said you're good-looking? Who has been flirting with my husband? Barbara had asked.

'Well, I think it was you – I hope it was you. Saying that, I'd had a few drinks. You and your sister do look similar,' Harold had said.

'You cheeky sod …' Barb had playfully but with some intent hit Harold hard before he could react.

Harold smiled at himself in the mirror and laughed. He

grabbed a taupe knitted jumper and headed downstairs. He flicked the kettle switch on and put a few slices of bread in the toaster, whilst finding his favourite mug for his coffee.

He sat at a small wooden table in the corner of the kitchen. He had a hot coffee steaming in front of him and a plate with two rounds of marmalade on toast. He ate the centre of the toast, leaving the crusts like a child. A layer of dust now covered a romantic book that he had been forced to borrow from a neighbour who had highly recommended it; he had no intention of reading this book. *Love and Lust*, the title read. He ran through these familiar words in his head. Yes, when he'd first met his wife (to be) Barbara, it was all about lust – that had started their relationship – but he eventually fell in love with her and they married. Lust and love are so similar and so far apart. He rubbed his chin recalling those words. He remembered the first time Barb had caught him out; she proceeded to throw a vase at his head. After six hours in A & E, they were sent home. Barb apologised the whole night, so much so that Harold had told her to stop saying sorry. He then felt more guilty than he had before she'd hit him. He rubbed his hand over the scar on his chin, where the vase had struck him all those years ago.

# CHAPTER TWELVE
# HAROLD
# EIGHT DAYS BEFORE

In the corner of his eye, he could see it moving again; if he blinked, he would miss it. It had at least four legs and a long tail, and it was speedy. It stopped abruptly. Harold sat still. The last time he had moved his head around too quickly, not only had he jolted his neck, again, but he'd also made the creature disappear. Patience was the key. Harold was retired and had all the time in the world. He could afford to wait, but patience wasn't his strongest quality; he'd never been a patient man. The creature was on the move again, and it was lightning fast. Harold could just about see it in his peripheral vision. It darted to the skirting board, and Harold turned quickly.

'Ouch, my God damn neck,' he shouted.

He looked down at the skirting boards and around the room, but he was left disappointed – the creature had vanished.

'Next time,' Harold angrily mumbled to himself. 'Next time, I'll get you.'

# CHAPTER THIRTEEN
## JUDE

Jude longed to have his old routine back; he didn't feel right without a plan. He'd been on the road for four days. He'd slept in his car twice and had stopped and stayed in two different hotels, including the quirky little Bournemouth Hotel. He contacted his old pal Ryan and they met up for a few drinks in Bournemouth; they drank far too much ale again. But luckily, Jude managed to convince Ryan to look after Dylan for a few weeks, whilst he worked out what he was going to do. He decided he had to go home and call the police. But first, he was going to visit Livewell care home, as he had someone he needed to see.

'Hi. I'm here to see Elizabeth Beecham,' Jude said to the rosy-faced lady, who was sitting at the front desk in the main building of Livewell care home.

'Okay, one minute,' the lady said raising a hand, whilst she finished sending a text on her mobile.

Jude was flabbergasted. He looked around; no one else was around to see her playing on her phone – just him. He took in his surroundings whilst he waited for her to finish texting her friend or whoever. The walls were all pale, the same colour as the old fragile people he'd seen walk past so far. The smell was pungent, a mixture of disinfectant and old, stale skin and somehow mixed up with a musty cat smell. He was glad he wasn't related to Elizabeth and especially glad he wasn't the person paying for her to stay here. There must be better care homes than this, surely.

He turned around as he heard a sudden crashing sound. A young blonde-haired lady was helping a poor elderly chap who was looking down at a cup of tea or coffee he'd just dropped – he just stared at the floor and waited for the girl to clean it up. Jude offered to help the poor girl, but she said she was okay. The old chap just held his hand out waiting for her to carry on holding his arm, so he could continue to walk wherever they were going. As they walked past Jude, the girl smiled at him. He could quite possibly be the only male under 70 she would see today, Jude thought.

The red-faced lady at reception looked down at a schedule of visitors for the day. 'What is your name?' She asked.

'Mr Beecham,' Jude replied.

'Her son – I didn't know she had a son,' the lady said. 'I can see the resemblance actually; it must be the nose.'

'I'm not sure if that is a compliment or an insult but yes, I'm her son – people have always said we look alike.' Jude couldn't believe how easy this was.

The lady shuffled about in her chair. 'Your mum hasn't got any visitors down for today. Have you visited her before? Do you want to book a time slot now?'

'Have I visited my mum before? Are you being serious?' Jude said. 'Look, I can see you're new or something, but Miriam normally cares for my mum. She just walked past – let me call her and see what's going on …'

'No, Mr Beecham, don't do that – there is no need. Let me give your mum a call and let her know you're here.'

'She does know, but that would be kind of you. I'll take a

seat over there.' Jude pointed into the corner and tried to look annoyed as he marched away from the reception desk. He stomped his feet all the way over to a TV set in the corner of the room. He took a seat on an off-red, overused sofa. He fought the urge to sniff or ask for some disinfectant to start cleaning it, and opted to sit on its edge. He made a mental note to himself to put some fragrance on when he got back in his car. He shuffled to try and get comfortable. The springs in the sofa were protruding through the leather and jabbing him in the legs and arse wherever he sat. He picked up a catalogue from off the adjacent coffee table and stood up to smack one of the springs back down. Just then, he heard some distant noise and looked up at the lady at reception. Her head was hunched over looking at her mobile phone again. He raised both of his hands above his head ready to strike the springs.

'Todd – well I never. It has been such a long time.' Jude dropped the catalogue and turned to see Elizabeth looking at him.

# CHAPTER FOURTEEN
## JUDE

Back at school, it was her kind eyes that Jude had always been drawn to. She could easily keep the attention of the whole class with one look, especially the boys. Jude had never thought about this until recently but her glittery blue eyes were beautiful, even now as she sat opposite him in the care home. She looked old, and yes, terribly frail – she had had to be guided to him by a nurse as she held tight to a Zimmer frame – but as she talked about the past, about school and being his teacher, her eyes still sparkled every time she smiled.

'You were always my favourite teacher,' Jude said. 'I don't mean to sound like a suck-up or cliché but you actually were.'

'And you always knew how to say the right words, you little charmer – I remember you talking your way out of trouble on more than one occasion. I bet you have the gift of the gab with all the ladies,' Elizabeth smiled, her eyes sparkling.

Jude half smiled back and looked out towards the window, scratching his stubbly chin. Relationships had never come naturally to him, and he was happy to change the subject.

'I might be old but I'm not stupid. I don't get too many visits these days, especially from my boy, Todd,' Elizabeth said.

'I'm sorry to have used his name …' Jude tried.

'Be quiet – let an old lady have her say,' Elizabeth said, her eyes narrowing. 'I don't get many visits from Todd, as you know. So, when a young, handsome man turns up and pretends to be my son to visit me – a young man who I used to know fairly well but one who has never visited me and I wouldn't expect to visit me, but here you are, turning up out of the blue in this God damn awful place – then I know he is here for a reason. Let's cut the small talk. Stop the charm act and you tell me exactly why you're here and what you really want.'

'I'm sorry that I haven't …' Jude hesitated. 'I know you said no small talk. Okay, the reason I'm here is Harold.'

'No, no I won't. I can't talk about him …' Elizabeth struggled to get up. Tears ran down the lines of her once youthful and still elegant face.

'Elizabeth, please sit back down and talk to me. We can talk about something entirely different – I didn't come here to upset you,' Jude pleaded.

Elizabeth wiped away the tears with the cuff of her charcoal grey cardigan and settled back down into her seat.

'Okay, I'll talk, but only because I have nothing better to do,' she said. 'I had managed to forget, but you know. Well, you don't, but I'd put this drama to the back of my mind.'

'I'm sorry to have upset you …' Jude began.

'Hold your horses,' Elizabeth said, putting her hand up just like the rude receptionist had done to him. 'Right, where was I? Here we go. I know. Now I'm thinking about them all again because of you. I'll tell you something: time is a funny thing. When you are young you never can have enough free time to do what you want to do – I think they call it "me time" these days. When you are young you are so busy having to work to pay for all those important bills. You dream of retirement, you wish you had more money to go on holiday, to play sport, to start a new hobby or just socialise with your friends.'

Jude nodded, but he was getting annoyed that she was moving off subject, but he also wanted to show he understood. 'Yes,' he said, and continued to nod.

'Then you get old, you don't work anymore and you're too old for sports. You've either had a knee or hip replacement and you are knackered. If you were a horse you'd be shot. No, not with a human; no, that is inhuman. And friends – what are they?' It was a rhetorical question and was shortly followed by Elizabeth laughing. 'I can see your face and that you think I'm merely evading your choice of subject. You may well be right, but I do have a long-winded point. What I'm trying to say is, with all this brilliant free time, I have lots of time to think. I try my best to keep busy – I do have hobbies like knitting and crosswords and these help me to avoid thinking of the past, all my past sins. But today, for the rest of the day once we've finished, I'll go back to my room and all I will do is think and I will cry and then I will cry some more. I think about Harold and my son, because you brought this subject up. So, anyway, that was my point. Let's talk.' Elizabeth looked at Jude. Her eyes this time didn't sparkle, and all the light had disappeared. She stared blankly at him. 'What is it that you want to know about Harold?'

'Why did you choose Harold? You had a partner and you were happy as far as everyone could see, including myself, so why, why did you and Harold have an affair?' Jude asked.

'You were a boy. What would you know?' Elizabeth said. 'He had an aura. Some men do. You have charm but it's not the same – it's not an aura. He was masculine, he oozed authority, yet he was charming. Do you have a girlfriend or a wife? You are old enough to be married by now.'

'Thanks. Well at least one of us has charm,' Jude said and smiled.

'I guess not then. Don't be offended please,' Elizabeth said. 'Anyway, he wanted to know us. Not just me, but he wanted to get to know my son as well. I was an unwed mum and at the time that was less common – it was looked down upon, not like it is today – it was completely different. Yes, I was seeing someone, but Todd didn't even know his dad.'

'But you knew he was married, right? Jude asked. 'What did his wife think of you spending so much time with him?'

'I never spoke to her and in fact I never saw her. Well, except on the one occasion.'

Jude could see her shudder as she had said 'one occasion', but he was afraid to push her too hard. 'Well, didn't this come across as a little strange that you only saw her once?' Jude asked.

'Why would it? It wasn't me who Harold was interested in really, now was it,' Elizabeth said.

'So, what really happened to Todd?' Jude asked.

'It's a long story,' Elizabeth said.

Jude left the Livewell care home with the answers he'd been after, even if they weren't what he was expecting to hear. He did remember to find his trusty bottle of fragrance when he got back in the car and douse himself all over with it. Driving away, he could still smell musty cat. Dylan would be ashamed, he thought.

# CHAPTER FIFTEEN
# HAROLD
# SEVEN DAYS BEFORE

As time passed and Harold had grown older, he'd lost contact with all his old friends or they had passed away, except for one. He had no children and his wife had deceased. He missed her dearly; he thought about her every day. He was alone and he felt alone. Each day, he tried to keep his mind active and to get some exercise. Most of the time, this was as little as walking to the shops, but he thought this was better than driving. It gave him a chance to stretch his legs and breathe in some fresh air.

Today, he'd walked to the local butchers and to a convenience store. He'd bought one box of teabags, a packet of chocolate digestives (his favourite) and two on-the-chunky-side beef steaks, not too thick mind as otherwise he found them a nightmare to cook. He preferred his steaks fairly well done, not on trend these days, especially with a few chefs who had previously refused to cook him well-done steaks. In the past, as in a few years back when he still went to restaurants, he had tired of the looks of sympathy – he didn't want their pity. If he mistakenly bought the steaks too thick, he ended up with them a little bit burnt on the outside and nearly blue in the middle. He always ended up having to put them back in the pan and then the rest of his dinner had gone cold by the time they were cooked. That's why he loved the butchers: he could ask for the cut he wanted. He never needed much at the shops as he went almost daily and Jane would drop off some fresh bits every few days. He was lucky to have her, he knew he was, but he tried not to make too big a deal out of it with her – too much praise might go to her head. And as always, he grabbed his daily paper and had already completed the three sudoku challenges from easy to very difficult, and it was only late morning.

It was 11.30am and Harold sat downstairs swaying back and forth in his antique wooden rocking chair. The chair itself was an heirloom passed down in his family through the generations. His great-grandad had made it for his wife, Harold had been told, but there had been many different variations of how the rocking chair ended up being a part of their family. One such story was his great-grandad, who worked in a farm as an extra pair of hands when he was a teenager, had come across the chair in an abandoned house on the land. The story goes he was told he wasn't needed by the farmer who was struggling for cash, and didn't have money to be throwing away. Harold's great-grandad was cheeky and asked if he could take the chair, but the farmer told him to do one. His great-grandad went back a few days later and stole it. The farmer never noticed it was missing or never said anything if he did.

Yesterday, Harold had painted his spare bedroom in cobalt blue. He'd decided to turn it into a reading room. He didn't have much need for a spare room anymore – he never had any guests staying over. He'd kept a pull-out bed in there on the off-chance of having some company. He steadied the rocking chair but now impatiently tapped his knees with his hands and thought of the old books he'd retrieved from the attic. His idea was he now needed a bookshelf for his reading room, but he was only going to pick a select few books, his favourite titles. He was about to get up – he'd decided to go out and buy the shelf – when he heard a loud thump from upstairs. It sounded like someone had run into a wall. He froze; he couldn't get himself to move; he was afraid. He had left a window open in the bathroom upstairs. It was probably the football again – Lewis and his pesky friend playing truant. He shook his head as he headed up the stairs.

Before climbing the stairs, he'd grabbed his trusty old baseball bat out of the cupboard. He kept it in there for emergencies and just in case it wasn't the ball, he took it with him upstairs.

'I'm letting you know first, I'm coming upstairs. I'm a frail old man, so don't frighten me as I might have a heart attack. You'll be done for murder,' Harold chuckled to himself, a laugh of fear or a genuine laugh – he wasn't sure which one it was.

When he had finally managed to make it to the top of the stairs, he was a little out of breath. After a moment's pause, he then checked in every room. He couldn't see a ball and decided there definitely wasn't anyone upstairs. He was extremely thorough – he even checked in the cupboards. He sat on the tartan pull-out bed/sofa in the reading room. On the bedside table he saw a book that he didn't remember leaving out. A shiver ran down his spine; he instantly knew which book this was. It was covered in dust. He picked the book up, which was as light as he remembered, and wiped away the dust. In the back of his mind, he knew he shouldn't open this book – what would Barbara think? But he wasn't too surprised to see it again – he'd seen the creature; he knew the book was next.

He read the first paragraph of the book aloud: 'What we

do on earth, what we do every day, can been seen.' He continued to read it out loud. 'What we don't do can be heard. The day that we give in is a day lost. The one we know as Utal we shall offer sweat, bone, blood and life. The sacrifice.' He closed the book and threw it on the floor. 'Not again. I can't, I won't, do this all again.'

# CHAPTER SIXTEEN
# THE UTAL
# THE SCRIPTURE 1
# SUNDAY, 25<sup>TH</sup> APRIL 1915

The sea was unforgiving. The waves rocked his and everyone's boats hard and his uniform was wet and felt heavy. It had been a long and grim journey. General William Day held on tightly to his own version of the bible; his cold hands gripped his book close to his chest. His boat was fast approaching land. This is what he feared the most – the journey had been treacherous but what waited was far more terrifying. He would rather drown than get off the boat. He was part of the British Empire's army, as they began their amphibious invasion of the Gallipoli peninsula, in the dark of the night. Troops mainly from Australia, New Zealand and the United Kingdom were about to invade the Ottoman Empire.

'What we do on earth can be seen. What we don't do can be heard. The day that we give in is a day lost. The one we know as Utal we shall offer sweat, bone, blood and life. The sacrifice.' The General muttered the words again and again.

'No one can hear you, General. You can talk to me – no one will bat an eyelid,' the creature said.

'Everybody can hear me. You are not real. Everybody on this boat is real,' the General whispered.

'It doesn't matter; you'll all be dead in five minutes,' the creature cackled, as it climbed up the General's left arm approaching his shoulder.

'You don't know that,' the General's voice trembled.

'You know the truth, and this is why you hold on to the book, and yet you look a ghostly pale. You have read the truth, haven't you?' The creature whispered and spat every word in the General's left ear. 'Call it your bible. It is not, but that doesn't matter. What matters is what I tell you now. You must put this book, the Book of Truth, in your satchel – it will be safe there. But first, take out your army knife and give what is expected.' The creature crawled on to the bridge of the General's nose and looked at his eyes. The creature's own eyes were veiny, bloodshot and without eyelids, never blinking.

'You brainwashed me – why should I believe you? The General said. 'I don't want to believe you.'

'Thousands will perish on both sides,' the creature said. 'Very soon, one ear will make no difference – odd fingers, intestines and blown-off heads will lay in the dirt. These parts that once lay snuggled up as newborns in their mothers' arms, whole and precious and loved more than the world itself. All will lay abandoned, forgotten for eternity. But you can show me your trust now and make this sacrifice and you will make a difference to the world.'

The General's screams were drowned out by shouting and the start of shots being fired as his left bloodied ear fell on to the book.

Five minutes later, true to the creature's word, everyone

on the boat was dead, all shot as soon as they made it on to land. The satchel swayed with the waves inside the boat, the pages of the book blood-splattered. The sweat, bones and blood of the General's left ear sat between the pages – the sacrifice. As the General took his last breath, the pages illuminated for a brief moment in time and the next page of the book was formed.

# CHAPTER SEVENTEEN
## THE UTAL
## THE SCRIPTURE 2
## SUNDAY, 25<sup>TH</sup> APRIL 2015

Garner's skin felt itchy and tight and his bones ached all over. He was 22 years old and he couldn't remember a time in his life when he'd ever felt this exhausted. He knelt on the solid concrete floor and arched his back over the wooden toilet bowl, or the hole in the ground as he'd noted in his diary earlier. He'd arrived late last night. He'd spent the last two years travelling and had always tried to keep a daily diary, with the ambition to one day have it published. He gagged but nothing came up. He closed the wooden toilet seat and slumped his drained body on to it, before managing to haul himself up and limp over to his bed, which he immediately collapsed on to. He put his sick feeling down to jet lag. After spending the last six months in Australia, he had decided to fly out to Nepal. Yesterday was a long day; he'd spent the whole of it and half of the day before travelling. After one long-haul flight and a lot of bus journeys, he'd managed to make it to his rather basic but fairly clean hotel he was now staying in; but it was well worth it – the views alone justified the long journey. He didn't know much about plants or have an eye for greenery, but what he did know was the vastness and array of green trees, plants and surrounding nature and mountains were simply breathtaking.

In reality, Garner hadn't thought his trip to Nepal through entirely. He was travelling anyway and fancied a new adventure, but what he knew was he had an interest in mountain climbing, and he thought, what better mountain is there to climb than Mount Everest? Also, he was keen on the feeling of Zen and the peace and quiet associated with Buddhism – Tibet was a must. For now, he was in the Gorkha District, and apart from the aches which he'd managed to shrug off to get out of his bed and out of the hotel, he had a strange but unimaginable feeling of impending doom.

He spoke with two local men who told him in broken English they were in charge of all the tickets for any excursions. He wasn't sure if the rumble in his stomach was sickness or hunger, and kept trying to make his excuses to leave them and go to find somewhere to eat. After buying tickets for a cable-car ride and to see the Manakamana Temple, he finally sat waiting for some food in a small café. He'd ordered some of the plainest food he could find a picture of on the menu and a drink of a local herbal spiced tea. In all honesty, he really wasn't sure what food he had ordered; the photo looked like rice and a type of meat – what meat? He didn't know, but he was looking forward to finding out. He put his earphones in and tried to relax.

Garner took his backpack off and took out his book, a reminder of home, of different times. The book was strange – he knew this. For instance, no matter how many times he cleaned it, it was always covered in dust the next time he opened it. He wiped away the dust and opened the book. He never actually understood why his dad guarded it – that's why he'd taken the book on his travels, to piss his dad off mainly. The thought brought a smile to his face. He had certainly achieved his aim. When his dad had found out the book was missing and presumed his son had taken it, he left messages, emails, calls, you name it, all trying to persuade Garner to leave the book behind and come home. Garner couldn't understand why a book that when he was at home he wasn't allowed to touch when growing up because it was too God damn precious his dad suddenly wanted left discarded in the middle of nowhere. He had told his dad many times he'd thrown the book in the bin back in Victoria, Australia.

He wasn't certain whether he'd dreamt it but he was sure when he was in Victoria, he'd woken up one night confused and angry and decided he must bin the book, only to find it was in his hands when he woke up in the morning. But he was sure that was a nightmare or something, definitely an odd dream. The main reason he didn't understand the book was because it only had four pages. The first page said some silly line about blood and a sacrifice – utter nonsense, he thought. The next page had some funny drawing, and the following double spread of pages didn't have a word, only a number in the top-left corner, the number 100. He shut the book and went to put it back in his bag, but the sickness feeling had turned into a light-headed dizziness. He closed his eyes and stretched his arms high above his head. He brought his hands down and rubbed his eyes before opening them wide. He made a strange, muffled, high-pitch squealing sound and fell back off his chair. He looked around but no one had noticed, and nobody, more worryingly, had seen the ugly-looking creature sitting on the bridge of his nose. He swiped at it with both hands; they went straight through the creature's torso like it was invisible or didn't exist.

'Why don't you read the book?' the creature said.

Garner looked around again, and wondered why the hell no one else could hear this creature talking. He wiped the dust from the front cover of the book again and turned the page looking at the funny drawing. He noticed this drawing now sat on his nose. He hadn't felt too well – this must be an hallucination, he rationalised.

'Turn the page. Quickly – we haven't got all day; well, in fact, we haven't much time at all,' the creature demanded.

As Garner turned the page to look at the blank pages, he was shocked to see the words starting to appear: *Date: 25th April. Time: 11.56am* … He looked at his watch to see the time was 11.53am. 'What is going on?'

The creature's expression never changed. 'The bad news for you is you're about to die, but I have good news …'

'No, you aren't real; you don't know anything. How would you know that I'm going die? This is ridiculous.' Garner's stomach ached and he could feel all the colour draining from his face. He wiped his forehead and it felt cold and damp.

'The Book of Truth knows. You can read, can't you?' the creature cackled. 'You aren't a follower and you don't know what this book is capable of. But this book has fallen into your hands – I will give you a chance.'

'A chance? Garner said. 'But you're going to kill me you just said.'

'No, I said you're going to die – there is a difference. Your death has nothing to do with my presence. But let's get back to your chance: reincarnation.' A vintage-looking army knife appeared in the creature's three-fingered right hand. 'Give me your left ear before it's too late.'

Garner paused and then stuttered, 'But, but I'm alive … and my ear, you are …' he began. The floor started to lightly rumble. He looked around – he could see panic on everyone's faces. He looked down at the book to read

*Earthquake, Nepal.* He looked at his watch again – the time was now 11.55am.

'The sacrifice is needed now.' The creature's face had changed. It bared its sharp teeth and blood started to fill its eyes; for a moment its eyes looked almost human, showing fear. They looked like they had seen a million deaths.

The ground shook violently; things started to fall – people started to fall. Garner could hear screams everywhere.

'Now!' the creature screeched.

'No, never.' Garner closed his eyes and turned up the volume of his music. His eyes filled with tears; his ears filled with the words of 'Bohemian Rhapsody'. The words felt more real than ever. He was shaking with fear.

He felt an excruciating pain on the left side of his face, and opened his eyes. The creature's face was dripping with blood. As it held on to Garner's ear with one hand, it thrashed, cutting at his ear with the army knife in its other hand. Garner tried to grab at the creature's arms, but nothing; it was the same as when he tried to grab his torso – there was nothing to hold. He looked at the creature's fearful eyes again – tears of blood were flooding out. Garner put his fingers into the creature's eyes. He could feel the eyes, the eyes that never shut, and he pressed in. The creature screamed; the café shook brutally. Garner's feet couldn't grip on to the floor anymore. The ground cracked and opened up, sucking him and the creature into the depths of the earth.

After the shaking had stopped, the words started to fade and the book didn't illuminate. It vanished, leaving only a few specs of dust behind.

# CHAPTER EIGHTEEN
## JUDE

He indicated right and pulled into the nearest layby. Jude had been driving for only five minutes since he'd left Livewell care home, but was shocked and needed some time to collect his thoughts. He took a look through his notes and then typed a postcode into his satnav app on his phone. The address was the one Elizabeth had given to him.

He sighed as he noticed the time to the destination on the bottom right of the screen. 'Another hour of driving,' Jude agitatedly muttered to himself. He knew it wasn't very long, but he'd been driving a lot more than usual over the last week and was now a little fed up with it.

On the way there, he stopped at an off-licence, bought a chicken, lettuce, mayo and mustard sandwich, salt and vinegar crisps and a luminous blue energy drink. He didn't smoke but knew he probably drank a little too much, but even so energy drinks were his little treat; he needed the caffeine boost. On the drive he turned his music up loud. The journey went fairly quickly; he'd made it there in just under an hour. As he pulled up, he did think that Elizabeth may have stitched him up. What if this was just some random address? He grabbed his pen and notepad before closing the car door behind him. He double-checked he'd locked it. He looked around the neighbourhood. The street had around ten houses, four of which were boarded up. He had a little chuckle when he thought about his boarded-up window back at his house – who was he to judge other people? Although, he wasn't too confident his car would be in one piece when he got back to it. A mangled grey cat purred as it walked up to him and rubbed up against his legs. He shook his leg and gestured for the cat to disappear; he wasn't a fan of cats. He slowly walked up to 3 Holbert Crescent. He knocked at the door loudly twice and waited patiently. He rubbed his hands together; his palms were clammy – he felt anxious. He stood there for a long minute. He went to knock again as the door unexpectedly swung open.

A scruffy girl opened the door. She had tight, worn, blue denim jeans on and a stained, baggy black top with a hood. She was inside, but still wore the hood over her head, her greasy, curly brown hair protruding from the sides.

'What do you want?' she asked in a no-nonsense tone. 'You're clearly not from around here, are you?'

Jude was a little taken aback with how rude she was. 'I was looking for a Todd – does a Todd live here?'

'Who's asking?' she asked him.

'An old friend,' Jude tried.

'Sorry.' She scratched her chin and looked away from Jude. 'Nope, I don't recognise you.'

Jude was a little bit confused. 'Todd?' he said.

Elizabeth had shown him some photos of Todd when he was younger, happier times she'd said. Although they weren't friends at school, he did recognise him. He was a shy child, that's all he could remember. He couldn't remember ever talking to Todd.

She took her hood off; her curly mop of hair had hidden her features but Jude could see there was a definite resemblance. 'Yeah, some people know me as Todd, but the few people I'm close to call me Tiff,' she said.

'Well, hi Tiff. Can we talk? It's about that night.'

# CHAPTER NINETEEN
# HAROLD
# THE BOOK OF TRUTH
# IN THE EIGHTIES

'This is the scripture – we didn't write it,' Harold said.

'It's not because I don't believe or that I don't follow, it's just …' Elizabeth began.

'A weak believer is the worst kind of believer. You are no better than a non-believer,' Harold said. 'When life gets hard do you just give in? Is that it? Should we all just give in?'

'It's not that. Well, I …'

'Lizzy, I know it's difficult. I truly understand, but we can't choose, can we?' Harold said.

'You have a gift. The Utal comes to you and I'm proud that he has chosen my son, I really am. It's just a big ask,' Elizabeth said.

'We still have time and that we can be grateful for, but we must decide how and we need to set a date. Lizzy, you understand this is for the best, don't you?' Harold paused for thought. 'Todd – he's a quiet boy, isn't he. Does he have many friends?'

'He, well, he has a few. I know he's quiet but he has friends – he does!' Elizabeth said loudly.

'No need to get defensive. I wasn't implying that he doesn't have any friends.' He stopped talking for a minute, and there was an uncomfortable silence. He smiled, 'Does Todd like football?'

'I suppose so.'

'Good. Bring him over with you tomorrow after school; I'll have a surprise for him.'

Not long after Elizabeth left, Barb came home.

'I can smell her perfume – it's sweet, it's overpowering, it's disgusting,' Barb said. 'You are disgusting.'

'Who – you can smell what, Barb?' Harold asked.

'You know who. I can smell Elizabeth or Lizzy or whatever you like to call your latest bit on the side,' Barb said. 'I know more than you think. Lizzy this and that on the phone at night. I can hear; I am not oblivious to what is going on.'

'You have me all wrong. She, well she, we have similar interests. She is a friend and that is all,' Harold said, and shook his head. 'Really, I'm insulted.'

'You really are a pig, a pig in shit,' Barb said, and jabbed a finger into Harold's cheek.

Harold clenched his fists, swore under his breath and turned to walk away.

'Why don't you roll away, you pig. Pigs like to roll around in their own filthy muck!' Barb shouted.

He ran his hands under cold water, grabbed a bag of frozen peas from the freezer and then picked up a tea towel off the kitchen side. He shook his right hand and then wrapped it with the frozen peas with the tea towel secured around it. He looked down at Barb, who still lay unconscious on the floor.

# CHAPTER TWENTY
# THE WRITER

The writer's nib had run dry mid-flow; after dipping the quill, they continued to write. They finished the paragraph, looked back at what they had already written and read out their work aloud:

The Utal, for the majority, is the unknown, or for the few the Utal will only be seen when they have been chosen to make their final choice. For you, this is different: you are not page 100; you are not a sacrifice who has been chosen to save the fate of humanity every 100 years. You are more; you are the constant. You, as the holder of this title, must obey orders given to you directly from the Utal. You will surpass 100 years in age, and until all the demands have been actioned and the next constant is in place, you will continue to live out your sentence, your life. Your past and present failures have only worsened the failures of Scripture 2, in Nepal 2015.

The writer folded the paper neatly and wax stamped an envelope. Now it was ready to post.

# CHAPTER TWENTY-ONE
# HAROLD
# SIX DAYS BEFORE

The parcel he'd been waiting for arrived in the post in the morning, along with some other junk. Harold gently put the box on the kitchen top. As he looked for some scissors, he first drank his hot cup of coffee, which he'd struggled to keep his hands steady enough to drink, before he opened the box. He had made toast with marmalade but he couldn't stomach it – the smell had made him feel queasy. After struggling with the excess packaging, he finally managed to retrieve the pack of L-Dopa capsules; he was thankful for how quick the turnover of ordering items online was these days and how you could get your hands on pretty much anything you needed. His supply had only run out yesterday morning and he immediately ordered them before he forgot. He sat down and swallowed two capsules of his medicine with a glass of cold water as quickly as he could whilst rolling his neck from side to side, trying to ease the pain. He jumped – there was a knock at the door.

'I thought you were going to leave me out in the cold all day,' Jane said. She raised her eyebrows and smiled, before brushing past Harold and into his house.

'Ahh, yes, I forgot it was cleaning day today,' Harold said and blushed.

'Don't worry. I'll be out of your hair within the hour today – I've got a dentist appointment at 10.30,' Jane said.

Harold was quite relieved. He did like seeing Jane; he had known her since she was a baby after all. 'I have some writing to do today – I'll be upstairs,' Harold said. 'Just give me a shout if you need me.' He would normally spend the first half an hour with her just catching up on gossip, but he had plans for today and had genuinely forgot she was coming over.

'Oh okay. Are you not going to ask me how I am? Or why I am going to the dentist?' Jane asked.

'Yes, sorry. I hope it's just a check-up – we don't want your gorgeous smile ruined,' Harold joked, and then laughed.

'Yes, just a check-up today, and an appointment with the hygienist to make my smile even more shiny and gorgeous,' Jane laughed. 'Anyway, don't you worry about me. How are you feeling? Did you book an appointment to see your doctor?'

'Yes, he only had space for next week. I'll see Doctor Furlong next Monday at 9,' Harold said. 'Lewis – how is he? Enjoying playing football is he?'

'He's okay, yes – he seems to have a good friend called Jay,' Jane said. 'I know I mentioned he was in with a bad bunch, but I think he and Jay seem to be good pals now and they aren't causing any harm. They go out playing football everyday with the ball you gave him. He did mention he thinks it may be bothering you a little bit, as he's hit your fence a few times he said.'

'No, it's no problem. As long as he's okay now,' Harold said, and then gently cricked his neck.

'Anyway, I've asked him to come round later today to say thank you. Will that be okay for you?' Jane asked.

'Of course, Jane. You know Lewis is always welcome, anytime,' Harold said.

Jane finished up her cleaning. She'd spent the whole time chatting to Harold and he didn't get the chance to get away to write even one word. He waved Jane off from his doorstep, closed the front door and went up to his reading room.

'Follow me,' a voice said.

Harold heard the creature; he was sure he'd heard him – he could smell the dust. He looked around everywhere, but he couldn't see it. He felt dizzy and confused.

'I've seen you and I can hear you. Show yourself now!' he shouted. Then the dizziness turned to black, his knees buckled and he fell, hitting his head on the door frame on his way down to the floor, before hitting it again as he landed face first.

# CHAPTER TWENTY-TWO

The front door slammed so hard Jude felt the air rush past him; it was close to hitting him square on the nose.

'Tiff, open up, come on. What harm can it do to talk to me,' he asked. 'I'm not here to write your story. I'm here because … well …' Jude stopped to think. He needed to talk to Tiff; he had to convince her. He only had one chance. 'I'm here because I think, well, I think it has happened again. Only this time you can help, Tiff. I need your help.'

The door creaked and slowly opened.

'You best come in then,' Tiff said, and she walked into her kitchen. 'Would you like a tea or a coffee?'

'A black coffee and one sugar would be lovely. I'm parched – thank you,' Jude said.

'Come in then. Don't just stand there letting all the cold in,' Tiff said. Jude came inside. 'Well, hurry up and shut the door behind you,' she said.

Jude sipped at his coffee. He did ask for sugar, but the first sip tasted like there were about ten tablespoons in it. He looked up at Tiff, who was smiling.

'Okay, let's get straight to the point,' Jude said. 'I went to the care home to visit your mum today.'

Tiff coughed and spluttered her drink of hot coffee on her top. She slammed the mug down on a coaster, and the coffee spilt out on to the table. 'That bitch – I hope she's rotting in there.'

'She isn't a happy old woman, I can tell you that,' Jude said. 'She gave me her version of events on that night. I want you to tell me what really happened.'

'Her version?' Tiff said. 'Okay, what did she say happened?'

'Okay, this is what she said happened: first of all, she started a few months before the night,' Jude said. 'But to skip to the point, she said she'd been brainwashed by Harold over those months leading up to what happened. He'd convinced her she must follow the Book of Truth or the world will suffer – the world will end. Does this ring true so far?'

'Yes, I remember Harold and his lies and his crazy ranting and that stupid book,' Tiff said. 'Carry on. What else did she say then?'

'She then told me about Harold, how he had convinced her that there must be a sacrifice,' Jude said. 'And the Utal had visited him and told him her son had been chosen. He convinced her that she was lucky and you were lucky.'

'The Utal. What a load of crap. Do you believe some mystical creature was talking to him? It beggars belief, it really does,' Tiff said, and wiped away a tear. 'And as for lucky, they must have been off their heads.'

'So, you remember them talking about the Utal?' Jude asked.

'Oh yes, I remember, and I remember how they both tried to convince me that this thing was real. Can you believe my own mother wanted to kill me?' Tiff took a moment, Jude nodded and she carried on. 'They said I'd be reincarnated; they said this was the start of my journey, the beginning of my life. Ironically, to begin my life they wanted to kill me first.' Tiff cried and laughed at the same time. 'I'm not sure I can do this. I'd put all this behind me until you arrived.'

'I understand. Shall we stop for now? Jude asked. 'I could come back later and try again, if you would like to talk again later today or tomorrow?' Jude tried.

Tiff had her head in her hands and didn't say anything. Jude waited. After a few minutes she got up and picked up a box of tissues. She wiped away her tears and blew her nose. 'Do you know what they did to me?' she asked.

'I've heard your mum's version,' Jude said.

'Let's see if she told you the whole truth,' Tiff said. 'They strapped me to a bed, restraining me by my wrists and ankles. They made me swallow loads of drugs and then gagged me with some old rag so I couldn't scream, so I couldn't spit the drugs out, so I couldn't be sick. And if I was sick I'd choke and die – good result for them either way. They told me the Utal will visit me. And they read together from their silly book. I looked at my mum for help. I could see tears welling up in her eyes, but then she just looked at Harold. I could see him take her by the hand and they just kept chanting about blood, sweat and bone. I thought I was going to die; I thought this was the end. Can you really understand how it would feel to die in this way, with your mum betraying you in the most evil of ways possible? Can you? She was supposed to protect me – that's what mums are meant to do,' Tiff sobbed.

Jude had gone pale. Elizabeth was vague on the details she told him. She was honest enough to say she'd been convinced to sacrifice her own son, but she wouldn't say any more. She had written this address, the one he now sat in with Tiff. She passed the address to him and told him to put it in his pocket safely, and then got up and shouted for a nurse. She had started shouting for help, repeatedly. Jude tried to calm her – he put his hands on her shoulders and said everything would be okay. But she then screamed even more, saying he was touching her inappropriately and that he wasn't her son – he was a liar, he was a fraud, he was here to hurt her, so he left the care home sharply.

'I can't do this – you need to leave!' Tiff started to shout, like her mum had shouted at him. 'Get out – go!' She pushed at Jude, making him get up. 'Go on – go. Don't come back.'

Jude half jogged out of the house; he narrowly avoided the door hitting his backside on his way out. He drove to the next road, stopped the car, pulled out his phone and played back the conversation. He'd had it on record since the moment he'd first knocked at Tiff's house. He then got his pad of paper out and a pen and wrote down every last word.

# CHAPTER TWENTY-THREE
## ARTHUR MORETON

Their relationship began shortly after the Second World War had finished. Arthur was 5 years old and on the thin side. He wasn't malnourished but did look ill – he wasn't though. And he was small in height even for his tender age. Throughout the war, his grandparents had taken care of him; his dad was at war and his mum had died giving birth to him. He didn't remember much about the war or his early childhood except for how strict his grandparents were with him. He had the feeling they wished he would disappear and that his mum, their daughter, would magically come back to life. They never said this and would often tell him how much they cared about him, but deep down Arthur was sure this was how they really felt.

The war ended and everyone celebrated, and then they waited and waited for his dad to come home; he never did. After a week had passed, their worst fears were realised when Harold knocked at their door. His dad, Henry Moreton, had struck up a friendship with Harold over their years together fighting the Germans and their allies. In the years to follow, Arthur had listened to Harold tell him the same old stories of his heroic dad again and again. He had heard many times how his dad Henry died on their last battle. He'd died on the battlefield but he'd died a hero trying to protect others. Arthur had never known either of his parents. Through guilt or pity or something, he couldn't quite understand why Harold kept in touch; throughout Arthur's childhood, they didn't live close to one another. But they stayed in contact as pen pals and as Arthur grew older and moved away from his grandparents' house, Harold would come and visit him on more and more of a regular basis. Harold wasn't a father figure as such, but he was more someone he could talk to, someone who didn't cast any judgement, or so this is what he used to think. Arthur had grown older and was now in his mid-70s, and with Harold being in his 90s their ages seemed closer than ever, but their age was the only thing that was close.

Since his near break-up with his wife back in 92, Harold hadn't blackmailed Arthur exactly, but he felt he'd taken advantage of him. When things had got really tough with his wife, he'd confided in Harold as he always had done, and he'd mentioned maybe it was inner guilt for the way he behaved. He accused his wife of all sorts of things he knew she hadn't done. He told Harold about a night he'd nearly cheated on his wife ten years ago at a work party with a younger woman; the woman who worked at the bar had flirted most of the night with him. She gave him free drinks and before he left for home, she gave him her number – he took it and smiled. He thought about calling her many times but didn't; but he was ashamed of himself and felt guilty about his thoughts. Shortly after this, Harold would give him silly jobs to keep his mind busy, but he'd jokingly say, 'if you don't do it, I'll tell your wife'. He could never quite tell if Harold was joking or if he was being serious, so he'd do these menial jobs just in case.

The years had passed and these days he was used to hearing from Harold more infrequently. There could be a few months or even a year or two could pass and then his phone would ring or more often than not he'd receive a letter, like today:

Dear Arthur,

I'll start with the usual small talk. I hope you and your family are all well, etc. Moving on swiftly, my old mucker.

The boy I once knew would always love a challenge. I believe you are still up to a final request, even though nowadays you're an old man like me – well, you'll never be as quite old as me but you are certainly getting on.

These days we never know who is reading what we are writing. The FBI, the Russians or China, or some other form of intelligence.

Okay, enjoy your post today and don't let your wife open it (wink, wink).

All the best, your good friend Harold.

'Friend? Ha!' Arthur said and laughed. He then screwed up the letter and threw it into the bin.

# CHAPTER TWENTY-FOUR
# JUDE

Entering the building hadn't been as difficult a task as Jude had imagined; it had in fact been really easy. He'd even managed to park in what was once and still felt like his parking spot. He was in the car park outside his old office.

He braced himself, held his head up high and then walked inside.

'Hi, Allan,' he said without looking at him. He walked down the central walkway through all of the desks. He kept his head high and didn't look at any of his old colleagues. He especially didn't want to see who sat comfortably at his old desk.

He firmly knocked on Mr Tomkins' office door. He could see him through the blinds, and he saw Mr Tomkins clock him and immediately panic – he could tell he had startled him. He wondered if Mr Tomkins would pretend that he wasn't there, even though they could clearly see each other.

'Er … come in … I suppose!' Mr Tomkins shouted. Jude opened the door and walked in. 'You know you shouldn't be here; I have a good mind to, well, I should call the police really,' Mr Tomkins said.

'Go on then. Shall I take a seat whilst you're on the phone,' Jude asked in a sarcastic tone.

'No, don't take a seat. I mean, I'm not calling the police, well not yet anyway. But don't get settled. What do you want?' Mr Tomkins asked.

'I have some news. You know the job, the one you really wanted me for, the one which you'd gone out of your way to employ me for. You got it? Surely. To write about the news – that job.'

'Enough of the sarcasm,' Mr Tomkins demanded. 'You know how much I appreciated you as a journalist. My hands were tied; I didn't have a choice. If you had only come to me first, before writing anything about Harold, I could have warned you.'

'I would have still wanted to go to print,' Jude said.

'The key difference is without my approval it wouldn't have been printed. Anyway, what do you have for me?' Mr Tomkins loudly demanded.

Jude intertwined his hands and stretched out his arms so his bones clicked. 'Okay, hear me out first – don't dismiss me straight away,' he said, and then he thought for a moment. He was too late to ask that question, as he'd already been dismissed from his role. 'It's about Harold's past. He isn't the man you think he is …' Mr Tomkins cut Jude off mid-sentence.

'No, I've heard enough. We, I mean the *Gazette*, can't risk another story being printed about him, we just can't. It's not worth the trouble it will cause.'

'He's crazy, he's …' Jude attempted.

'Get out – you don't work here.' Mr Tomkins opened the door wide. Everybody turned around to see; everybody was looking and listening to them.

'He's part of a cult; he's the leader,' Jude said, and looked around seeing every one of his old colleagues staring at him, as though he was the crazy one. And bloody Bella was sat comfortably at his old desk. He felt enraged.

'Go on, go. You don't work here anymore,' Mr Tomkins said as loud as he could without shouting.

'He tried to kill a child! And not just Jay – he's done this before.' Jude instantly regretted what he said because if people thought he sounded mad before, they certainly would have no doubts about it now.

'Okay, that's enough. I'm calling the police.' Mr Tomkins walked back into his office and grabbed his phone.

Allan came over to Jude and held him by his arm. Smiling Allan thought he was a peacemaker; he thought he was in the right. Jude couldn't believe it.

'Come on, Jude. Let's get you out of here. Nobody wants any trouble and nobody wants a scene; this isn't a pantomime,' Allan said and smiled.

Jude brushed Allan's arm off him and walked off, heading for the exit.

'Fuck off, smiley Allan,' Jude said, and fiercely slammed the door behind him.

He walked over to his car, opened the door and slammed it shut. He sat down and put the key in the ignition. He took a moment to gain back his composure, to breathe. He felt angry but more than that he was frustrated with putting himself in a position to look silly again. He needed more information, more evidence, and next time he wouldn't go to Mr Tomkins, who had no backbone. He was ready. He reversed out of his old parking spot; in his rear-view mirror he saw the blue car again. He put his foot down and spun the car around as fast as he could – he was going to catch the person following him. He looked ahead and from side to side; the blue car was nowhere to be seen. Was he being paranoid or was someone following him? He wasn't sure anymore.

# CHAPTER TWENTY-FIVE
## ARTHUR

He shouted 'Dial Harold!' at the car. Luckily, it worked first time, for once, he thought, which helped stop his anger from boiling over. He had his foot on the gas; he was sure Jude hadn't seen where he'd gone and was as sure as hell he wasn't going to let him catch up with him.

'Hello, Arthur. How lovely to hear from you,' Harold said. 'You sound like you're driving. Should you be calling? Isn't it dangerous to be on the phone whilst driving? I think at your age you should know better by now.'

'It's hands-free,' Arthur said abruptly, trying his best to keep his already thinning patience. 'Having me follow someone is probably a tad bit more dangerous, do you not think?'

'Keep your hair on, old chap,' Harold said, and Arthur heard him follow up the remark with a laugh.

'Is that supposed to be funny?' Arthur asked. 'You know this is a sore subject for me.' When he and his wife were having a rough patch, he lost all the hair on his head through stress, and it had never grown back. 'You know I'm doing you a favour, right?'

'Okay, I won't mention the hair again,' Harold said. 'It's an easy job – I did the difficult part. I had his car bugged and I organised this to be paired with the satnav. Just don't need to get too close. You're only supposed to frighten him, not date him or run him over,' Harold laughed again.

'Don't be ridiculous and that was a mistake – I didn't mean to drive at him, you know I didn't.'

'Old age that is, Arthur,' Harold said. 'Life can get confusing. Semi-skimmed milk or whole – which is green and which is blue? The brakes or accelerator – left or right? An easy mistake, I understand.'

'Piss off, Harold, you patronising sod,' Arthur said. He'd never spoken to Harold like that before; it felt good.

'Wow, very good,' Harold said. 'I didn't think you had that in you. But don't forget to keep to the task and say hello to your lovely wife for me, will you.'

The call ended and Arthur's heart hurt – he thought maybe he should tell his wife. Nothing happened, he didn't cheat on her and it was such a long time ago. But then again, what was the point of bringing up something that never happened and was so far in the past.

'Call Harold!' Arthur shouted again.

'What do you want now?' Harold answered.

'I think you have more to hide than me,' Arthur said. 'This is the last job I'm going to do for you and you're not going to say anything to my wife or even mention her again. Because if you do, I can promise you Jude won't be the only one looking into your past. You got it, old chap?'

'It's taken your whole life but I'm proud of you,' Harold said. 'Well done – sticking up for yourself at last. And don't worry, this is the last job. I had already told you it was.'

'Okay, good,' Arthur said. His heart thumped and he hung up on Harold for once.

# CHAPTER TWENTY-SIX
# YOUNG JUDE
# GROWING UP

The noise was unbearable. He could hear her banging utensils and smashing pots and pans around in the kitchen; she was slamming one door and then another and it had woken him up yet again. She'd always said to him to make sure he got to sleep nice and early as sleep was what healed your body and brain, and this helped you to grow and develop, and it was especially important for a child. But the problem was her. How could you sleep if you lived with a wild animal bashing into the walls and banging about the cupboard doors? Jude was rudely woken up almost every night. He was 10 years old and his teachers would ask him regularly at school why he looked so tired. Why was he yawning in classes? They would ask if everything was okay at home, which he always replied with a yes, and for him it was; this was his normal. He didn't know any different; this had always been the way. This time it was different. It wasn't the first time and it wouldn't be the last but it was always worse when he came back. He hadn't seen him yet but he was back.

Jude listened intently. It was 2 in the morning. He rubbed

his eyes and face; she'd been screaming and shouting and there was no chance he could sleep – he was completely awake. He crept downstairs and sat outside the kitchen – the door was closed. The floor that led to the kitchen was tiled like the kitchen and felt ice cold. He shivered as he sat there in his paper-thin tartan pyjamas. His mum was on the phone chatting to her friend Marilyn, and was calming down.

'I don't need him – he knows I don't and that's why he acts the way he does,' Jude's mum, Mary, said. He could hear her talking on the phone about his dad. His mum never said anything nice about his dad. But why would she? Jude didn't even know his dad – he just turned up when he felt like it, or so it seemed, he thought. Jude guessed what Marilyn might be saying on the other end of the phone line, like: 'You are right, Mary; you always are and he doesn't deserve you. You are my hero'. He laughed and then quickly tried to muffle it; he didn't want to be caught out of his bedroom at this time of night. She would definitely start screaming and shouting again, but this time he'd be the target. She hadn't heard him and he could hear her carrying on chatting to her friend – he could relax momentarily.

'I'm scared you know, Marilyn,' Mary said. 'I really, I'm … I don't know what to do.'

This caught Jude by surprise. He'd never heard his mum say she was scared, ever. Scared of what? Was he abusive to her?

'You don't know what he's like,' his mum shouted, and slammed the phone down.

The conversation had stopped abruptly and he heard his mum smash the phone down repeatedly and then start walking around the kitchen. He got to his feet as fast and as quietly as he could. He managed to make it back up to bed without being heard, but the thought of his mum being scared kept him up almost all of the rest of the night. Was she scared of his dad and if so, why? What could he have done that would scare her? Jude thought. He was angry and wanted to confront his dad, and he would next time he saw him – that was his plan.

# CHAPTER TWENTY-SEVEN
# HAROLD
# FIVE DAYS BEFORE

He blinked a few times, raised his eyebrows and then stretched his jaw until it clicked and crunched. Harold put his hand to his face, felt his left cheek just under his eye and then looked at his hand, which was warm and slightly wet – it was covered red with sticky blood. He felt groggy, like he'd woken up from an almighty bender. He then managed to manoeuvre his tired body enough to be able to sit upright against the sofa bed.

'Bloody Utal,' he muttered under his breath.

By the time he had been able to drag himself to the bathroom, sort his face out, have a shower and get changed, it had turned dark outside. He wondered how long he'd been out; he worked out it must have roughly been four or five hours. His shakes had returned. He couldn't remember if he'd taken his pills, so he took another two to be on the safe side. He heard the doorbell go off downstairs. He suddenly remembered Lewis was supposed to be coming over this evening. The bell rang again.

'Wait one moment, please!' he shouted. 'Be patient – I

can't move as quickly as I used to be able to.'

By the time he'd finally made it down the stairs and opened the door, Lewis was already halfway back up the driveway.

'Hi, Lewis – come back, boy!' Harold shouted.

'Oh, sorry – I thought you were out,' Lewis said, as he turned back around to see Harold.

'No, I'm just old – it takes me a while these days to get to the door. You'll be old one day too, son,' Harold said, whilst picking up the post and placing it on the side table.

'Old maybe, but not that slow. I'll never be that slow,' Lewis laughed.

Harold laughed too. 'Don't be cheeky. Come inside – you'll catch a chill out there.' Harold rubbed his hands together imitating how cold it was.

'My mum said I should come and apologise to you for kicking the ball towards your house all the time, like, because it's the ball you got me and it's not nice and, well …'

'And, well what? Don't be afraid to say what you're thinking,' Harold said.

'Well, you've already said it, I guess – because you're old. And you might get frightened and shit. Also, sorry Jay keeps sticking his finger up at you. Thanks for not saying anything to my mum.'

'There you go, boy – that wasn't too difficult. Anyhow, your mum doesn't need to know everything and you didn't need to come and apologise to me. I'm just glad you're well and making friends now.'

'Yeah, I'm fine. I mean, I've always had friends. It's my mum – she exaggerates about everything,' Lewis said.

'She said you were falling into the wrong crowd, you just weren't yourself, you were withdrawn,' Harold said. 'But you seem okay to me, boy.'

'I had a few fights, that's all. It's no big deal. You look like you've been getting into more fights than me. What happened to your eye?' Lewis asked.

'What have I said about being cheeky? It was just a little slip, nothing more,' Harold said.

'Anyhow, I should go. Jay's waiting outside for me to play footy. We'll try not to kick it over your fence again this evening,' Lewis said. 'And I'll tell him not to swear at you.'

'Okay – enjoy. I was going to ask if you wanted to help me with something, but maybe next time?' Harold said.

'Tomorrow's good, and oh yeah, sorry I didn't make it to yours yesterday after school,' Lewis said.

The door swung shut. Harold stood in his hallway, more confused than ever.

The words echoed around the room: 'You silly old fool.'

# CHAPTER TWENTY-EIGHT
## YOUNG JUDE

He threw his duvet on the floor in temper and slowly got up and out of his bed. The racket the engine was making had woken Jude up and annoyed him. He looked out of his bedroom window and could see an old, green, slightly rusted Volvo parked outside his house. Even before he'd even seen the car, he knew straight away it was his dad's. It was early morning and he'd hardly had any sleep, and it was most likely his dad's fault, he thought. He jumped when his dad hit the horn of the car and held it down for far too long.

He opened his bedroom window as he heard his dad shout, 'Come on then, boy. Mum said I'm taking you to school today. Will you get a move on – I haven't got all day!'

'I'm not even dressed yet!' Jude shouted back down to his dad. 'I don't need to be there for at least another hour. You're too early – come back in half an hour.'

'That's your mum for you. Always confused,' his dad said. 'Come down, or you can walk to school.'

'I'll be down when I'm ready,' Jude said, slamming the window shut. His dad was already insulting his mum and he'd only been here a minute.

'Mum, did you tell Dad he could take me to school?' Jude shouted towards his mum's bedroom. He shouted it a few times with no answer. He looked in his mum's room and she wasn't there. He tried shouting downstairs and still there was no answer. He looked around and couldn't find her anywhere in the house.

He was still in his pyjamas, but ran barefoot out to his dad's car. His dad was smirking as Jude made it over.

'What you doing?' his dad said. 'Why aren't you ready to go? I'll take you in with you dressed like that if I have to.'

'Where's Mum?' Jude asked.

'Sleeping Beauty is probably in bed – too many nightcaps as usual. Have you checked her room?' his dad asked.

'No, she's not there. That's why I'm asking you. She was banging around last night and shouting. You have annoyed her like you do when you come back, like you always do,' Jude said. 'This is your fault.'

'Don't get smart with me, boy,' his dad said. 'Right, you need to go and get ready. Get some clothes on quickly. Don't shower – we haven't got time. You just go and put something warmer on and as quick as you can.'

Jude hesitated for a moment before he started to run back into the house. He could hear his dad bellowing, 'And put some shoes on, boy, and do it sharply!'

He grabbed the first clothes he could find out of his wardrobe and put his warm, charcoal grey duffle coat over the top. He squeezed into his black school shoes without even untying them. It was the look of fear on his dad's face when he was telling him to be quick that worried Jude the most; his face never gave much away. He picked up the spare keys from under the clay flower pot at the front of the house (his mum was always in so he didn't have his own set of keys himself – he was only 10 years old), locked the front door and ran and jumped into his dad's car.

Except the odd smirk which annoyed him, Jude found it difficult to read his dad. He always looked serious but never scared. They had been in the car for almost ten minutes and Jude had asked lots of questions, but his dad had barely answered any of them – he'd either nodded or grunted. Jude hardly knew his dad. He wouldn't see him for months on end and then suddenly he would appear out of the blue one day. He would move back in for a few months, they would play happy families and then he would disappear again. This pattern seemed to be on a never-ending repeat. His dad never seemed happy. Jude felt on edge when he was back and his mum was even more wild – she would be over the moon and dancing and playing music, and then suddenly be shouting and screaming, like she was last night.

'My school will wonder where I am if I don't go in,' Jude said.

'What?' his dad said.

'You should call them and tell them I'm not well. Do you have their number?' Jude asked, but he knew what his dad would say. There was no way his dad had the school number.

'Yes, okay – you call them,' his dad said.

'I can't call them. I'm 10 years old. They would ask to speak to you.'

'Okay,' his dad said.

Jude sat there confused. What does okay mean? Is he going to call them? He didn't understand his dad's answer. They sat in silence for another five minutes.

His dad pulled into a service station. 'Are you hungry? Do you want anything? Have you had breakfast?'

'Erm … yes, I'm starving. Can I have …' Jude tried to answer, but his dad walked off mid-sentence.

Jude sat in the car wondering why his dad was taking so long and felt really hungry now. He couldn't stop thinking about food; he hoped his dad heard him say yes. His dad slammed the car door shut as he got back in. Jude could instantly smell the coffee and, more importantly, the hot sausage rolls. His dad passed him a carton of fresh orange juice and one fairly good-sized sausage roll. They sat in silence and both finished their rolls before his dad started to drive again.

'I thought we were in a rush, aren't we?' Jude asked.

'You might not be so hungry later. Biscuit?' his dad asked, and pushed the packet towards Jude.

If Jude wasn't worried enough, he was even more concerned now. 'Shall I call my school?' Jude asked.

'You asked me to call. I've just called them,' his dad said.

'Oh okay. I thought … never mind,' Jude said, and half smiled. 'What did you tell them? What did you say was wrong with me?'

'You have been bouncing up and down like a yo-yo off the toilet all morning,' his dad said, with a serious face.

'Nice,' Jude laughed.

His dad smirked. 'Did you want a biscuit?'

'Mum says I shouldn't eat sweet things in the morning.'

'She's not here is she,' his dad said.

'Okay, go on then,' Jude said, and took two biscuits. 'I should be careful with my upset tummy though,' Jude laughed, and looked at his dad, but he was back to having that look of panic on his face again, the face Jude hadn't seen before until today. They sat in silence and his dad continued to drive.

# CHAPTER TWENTY-NINE
# HAROLD
# FOUR DAYS BEFORE

Harold sat agitated on his antique chair and rocked back and forth. Every so often he looked down in front of him where he'd now placed the book on the top of a set of nested tables. He'd decided his newly decorated room needed better heating. It was far colder upstairs; when reading, his hands felt icy and the cobalt blue he'd painted the room in was off-putting. He needed to redecorate the reading room, again; he needed a bland colour, something that was less distracting. So, he brought the book down and into the living room, and sat contemplating if he should read it. From past experience he knew this was a bad idea; he knew if he even read one word then his life would change, again.

He got up and walked into the kitchen to make himself a coffee, and shuffled around and ate a plum whilst he waited for his drink. He brought the hot mug of coffee into the living room, with a handful of chocolate biscuits.

The pages flicked over and over; thousands of pages kept changing – this in a book that only consisted of a few pages. Harold's hands were still full. He wanted to shut the windows but when he looked over at them, they were shut, and it was a mild day and not windy. There was no feasible reason for the pages to flicker. He felt nervous; he was scared.

His hands shook as he put down the coffee and biscuits. 'What do you want from me?' Harold asked, and looked down at the book. The pages stopped flicking, and unexpectedly it slammed shut. The Utal squeezed and crawled out of it and moved towards Harold.

'You know, Harold. You have always known,' the creature said.

Harold was frozen still; he couldn't move. He went to talk but his lips wouldn't move; he went to move his hands, but he couldn't. Inside his head he screamed – he felt paralysed.

The Utal had now crawled up on to Harold's torso and it sat on his shoulder and whispered in his left ear, 'What we do on earth can been seen. What we don't do can be heard. The day that we give in is a day lost. The one we know as Utal we shall offer sweat, bone, blood and life. The sacrifice.' The creature quoted the words from the Book of Truth.

Harold still couldn't talk or move. He stood still and remained incapacitated.

'Do you remember these words? Because you should do,' the Utal said. 'And now is the time we start a new chapter. You have failed me before, but I will give you another chance. Lewis will help you and now you must guide him.'

The creature had moved and was now sitting on the bridge of Harold's nose. This was the first time in many years that Harold remembered seeing the Utal's unblinkered eyes, staring at him, intimidating him. The fear he felt was a familiar feeling from the last time he'd killed somebody.

The Utal, as it had done so many times before, disappeared into thin air. Harold stood alone, not moving, frozen in fear, like he'd also done so many times before.

# CHAPTER THIRTY
## YOUNG JUDE

Jude's head and neck jolted as he woke up all of a sudden; the sausage roll that filled his stomach and the motion of the car had sent him fast asleep. He glanced at the time on the radio clock and it was approaching 8am. They hadn't been in the car that long but he had been woken up early and hadn't had much sleep last night. It was going to be a long day. His dad slowed the car down as they were driving down a bumpy lane; there were potholes all over the road, more holes than road itself, or so it seemed. Green trees and bushes started to enclose the road. His dad took a left that Jude didn't even see coming. The road was now more of a mud track, and they continued on this for five minutes before Jude could see a sandstone-coloured castle which looked like it had been converted into a house. The closer they got to the castle the smoother the road became. Either side of the road and surrounding the castle was beautiful with luscious lime green grass, dotted with little snowdrops and tulips everywhere. The car slowed until it gradually came to a complete stop. Jude looked at his dad, who was scratching his chin.

'Okay, we're here, son,' his dad said.

'Where are we?' Jude asked. He suddenly remembered he was angry with his dad and wanted to confront him. Why had he hurt his mum? Why was she scared of him?

'Come on, get out,' his dad said. 'It's a long story. No time to chat now though. Let's go inside.'

Jude was confused. It was like he had read his mind, but his dad must be talking about the castle.

As they walked over and got closer to the building, it didn't look as magnificent as it had from a distance. The castle house looked like it could do with some attention; it was by no means dilapidated, but it needed some love. They stood at the front of it and his dad started to play around with the door.

'Just knock and someone will answer,' Jude said.

His dad shook his head and pushed with his right shoulder on the old wooden door. It creaked and scratched on the stone floor underneath and opened slightly. 'No need – it's open,' his dad said. 'Come on, let's go inside.'

Jude watched his dad just fit through, with his slightly bloated belly getting a little squashed as he managed to get inside the castle. He followed and easily fitted through the gap.

'Hellloooo!' Jude shouted, and his voice echoed around the castle. The building had no furniture in it and felt cold and hollow. Nobody was here; nobody would have answered the front door; the building was abandoned.

'Shhhh!' his dad snapped, and turned back to face Jude. 'Don't do that again. Be quiet – no talking from now on and tiptoe.'

Jude was a little taken aback; he couldn't remember his dad ever shouting at him or telling him off. His mum would normally be there to defend him or tell him off instead of his dad.

He was taking in his surroundings, whilst he ran his left hand along the sandstone walls, when he heard birds tweeting. He looked up and there was no roof; he could see straight up to the sky and the birds flying up above him. Ahead of him, he could see a huge semi-circular atrium that broke off into another equally large room and a few smaller rooms. He followed his dad up an out-of-place, rusted, cold-metal spiral staircase. He bit his lip; he didn't particularly like heights and tried to not look down at the gaps between each step as he walked up. Thankfully for Jude, they didn't go right up to the top.

'Are you okay?' his dad whispered. As his dad turned around to check, Jude nodded without looking at him.

'Where are we going? No one is here – it's abandoned,' Jude said.

'Shhh. We're nearly there,' his dad said, as he put his finger to his mouth.

He remembered and tiptoed like his dad had told him to. They stopped at door number thirty.

His dad knelt down in front of him and spoke softly. 'Your mum is in this room. Now I need you to listen carefully to me, you understand?' his dad asked.

'Great – let's go in and get her and then we can leave this spooky place. We can take her home,' Jude said. He felt excited he was going to see his mum. He didn't normally but he'd been worried about her. He knew his dad would find her.

'I told you to listen,' his dad said. 'You are to wait here. I'll be a few minutes, okay?'

'Why?' Jude asked. 'I don't want to wait. It's scary out here; I don't want to be on my own. Please, Dad.'

'I'm not negotiating with you. Stay here and do not move – do you understand?' his dad said, pressing down on Jude's shoulders to reiterate his point.

Jude nodded and watched his dad slowly and carefully ease the door open. His lip trembled; he had tears running down his cheeks. He was scared on his own and scared of his dad, and didn't even know where they were. They could be anywhere. If his dad didn't come back, how would he get back home? But what was the point of going home if his mum wasn't there, he thought. He could see into the room – his dad had left the door ajar. He cupped his ears trying to hear if anyone spoke.

'I knew you'd be here. It had to be here,' his dad said. Jude could hear him perfectly; the words vibrated when anyone spoke, and the hollow empty castle almost echoed every word.

'Yes, dear. I think this place is as good as any,' his mum said. Jude breathed a sigh of relief – they'd found her. 'Do you not like it here, darling?'

Jude could see his dad pulling his collar and rubbing his hair with the other hand. 'Have you done anything I should be concerned about?' his dad asked.

'I said do you not like it here?' his mum repeated.

'We both have memories, love. This place changed us, I know. I can only say sorry so many times,' his dad said.

'Sorry doesn't undo the past though, does it, Liam,' his mum said. 'You made me this way. I was normal before. Well, you know I was normal before you did this to me.'

'I know no apology can change the past, Mary,' his dad said. 'But you can't keep punishing me and the boy for something that I did years ago. It's not fair on me and it's definitely not fair on the boy.'

'Not fair? Fair? Do you want to talk about fair to me?' his mum laughed or cried – Jude wasn't sure. 'On our wedding night, in this castle and in this room …'

'The boy's just outside this room. Come on, be fair. He's been through enough,' his dad said.

There was a slight pause. 'And my sister,' his mum said. 'You and my God damn sister in my wedding bed. And you think I should be quiet. Do you think our boy shouldn't know the truth about you? Is that fair? Is living a lie fair?'

'Mary! I said he is outside – come on,' his dad said.

'Anyway, you men are all the same. He'll turn out just like you. Mark my words,' his mum said.

Jude turned and stumbled, instantly hitting the wooden decks and scraping his knee against the floor, but he bounced straight back up and ran for the stairs. His fear of heights had almost disintegrated as he took two steps at a time on his way down. He just managed to keep his balance as he made it down to the bottom. He didn't look back as he ran out the castle doors, easily making his way through the gap. He looked back at the castle and ran towards the doors to close his parents inside. In that very moment, he was full of anger and hated his dad, but what his mum had said was worse – he hated her more. He went shoulder first, and screamed as he felt a sharp pain in his arm. He bounced off the door and instinctively grabbed his shoulder with his other hand. He could see blood seeping through his fingers.

'Mum!' he screamed.

# CHAPTER THIRTY-ONE
# JUDE
# PRESENT DAY

The dull beige wallpaper hadn't changed since he could remember, except it had started to peel in the top corners. Jude wondered why his mum had never thought to brighten up the room; her mindset wasn't the same as his. She wouldn't think of how a fresh lick of paint, or even some fresh beige, or, being slightly creative, another colour wallpaper, might give the room or the people sitting in it some more life or a happier mentality. He'd been sitting in his childhood living room for almost an hour; it seemed longer. The whole room, except for how it had aged, was the same as it was when he was a little child; the lavender and sweet lemon scent brought back a thousand memories. He daydreamed until has mum came back into the living room. He straightened his back, sat upright and waited for her to start. Who would be her target today? Most likely the usual suspects. His dad or himself?

'The problem with writing is, I would say, well, especially in your case, is you have to be objective,' his mum said.

'Unless you have the cold hard facts or you have evidence, which you don't. You can't just write how you feel or what you think happened. It's journalism, son – you're not writing fiction. Anyone can do that.'

'Anyone like you, do you mean?' Jude asked. He knew this would wind her up. He walked over to the window and could see the blue car again. He was now certain he was being followed. It was parked just that little bit too far away for him to make out who sat inside it. He got his phone out his trouser pocket – he was going to call the police.

'Not anyone, but in some ways yes, anyone,' his mum said. 'All I mean is fiction is making up a story. When you work for the paper, you can't go and make stories up. It's wholly unacceptable. There are repercussions for these types of action. Well, you would know best, dear. You're now feeling the consequences for your willy-nilly approach, aren't you, dear?'

Jude was used to his mum's passive-aggressive manner and her condescending tone. He used to bite back all the time, but he'd learnt it didn't get him anywhere. But sometimes he couldn't help it. 'Have you spoken to my dad recently?'

'No, not recently,' his mum said.

He knew full well she had spoken to him; his dad only called him when he'd been told to by her. 'Funny – he seemed to know a lot about what is going in my life for someone I rarely hear from.'

'He must have spoken to Marilyn or, you know, he has watched the news,' his mum said. 'Or better still, he's spoken to my sister. God knows …'

'My auntie, you mean. Shall we change the subject?' Jude said, instantly regretting his choice of topic. How she had changed it to his auntie was so typical of his mum. He put his phone back in his pocket; he couldn't put up with how his mum might react if he called the police.

'You brought her up,' his mum said, and smiled her passive-aggressive smile, the only one Jude had ever really known.

'I didn't, but that's not the point, is it?' Jude said.

'What is the point, dear?' his mum asked. 'I never know with you. I guess it's like your writing – there is no point.'

Jude bit his tongue before speaking. 'We all know this topic of conversation never ends well,' he said. 'And I'll choose to ignore you insulting my career.'

'What career?' his mum said, and tutted before she smiled again. 'Okay, you're right, dear, like usual. I'll go and make us another lovely hot cup of tea.'

'Thanks, Mum,' Jude said reluctantly. For the sake of ending the conversation, he let her have the small win. Her sarcasm and this very room he sat in had brought back his childhood memories. He knew his childhood was a walk in the park compared with others, like Tiff. He felt guilty complaining, so he tried his best to never moan to friends about his family. His mum loved him. She showed him affection differently to other parents and her shouting matches with his dad weren't easy and nor were her disappearances, but he always felt he had a mum who cared for him, although sometimes he found it hard to believe she did care.

He remembered hobbling into this living room – he must have been seven years old – after he'd fallen off the wall in the back garden and grazed his knee. His mum cuddled him and told him everything would be okay. She was kind in her own way. He remembered later that day his dad had made one of his surprise visits, and he overheard his mum talk with his dad about him.

'The little blighter came running in sobbing. He was

crying about a little scratch on his knee today,' she said. 'If you were his dad, maybe you could teach him to be a man.'

Those words still hurt today. Jude tried not to hold these little remarks she made against her, especially the ones she said thinking he couldn't hear her. But he struggled. She loved him, he knew that, but this was just one example of how insensitive she was. He'd held so many tears in since he'd heard her say he needed to be taught how to be a man. It was only when he'd moved away from home that he'd finally realised he was allowed to cry – men do cry. He swallowed hard and rubbed his eyes as his mum walked back into the room with the two teas. He was allowed to cry but didn't want her to see one tear.

'Are you tired, dear?' his mum asked.

'Yes,' Jude said. He could almost hear his mum roll her eyes at him.

# CHAPTER THIRTY-TWO
## ARTHUR

'These youngsters with their PlayStations and Netflix have no patience nowadays. Nobody uses their brain anymore,' Arthur said. He was mumbling to himself, sitting alone in his car.

He had thought about getting an app with a game of some sort on his phone to play, but you can't beat a good old game of solitaire with the actual cards – an app doesn't have the same feeling and emotion, he thought. He had also struggled to remember his password when he last went to install an app. After finally remembering and saving the password to auto recall it for next time, he actually had installed a poker game last week. The problem was he couldn't work out how to play the game. Today, he had real cards. He'd taken his seat belt off and sat twisted to one side with the cards laid out on the passenger seat, and he was playing his favourite game, solitaire.

Arthur couldn't believe Harold had somehow persuaded him into this one last job. There was always one last job, but this was on his way home and this time, this was it – no more. No more hiding his post from his wife, no more instructions and silly emails – this was it. He wasn't impressed when his phone started to ring. 'Yes, Harold,' he said, purposely trying his hardest to sound rude.

'Okay, enough of the attitude,' Harold said. 'What is he doing now?'

'I don't know. You just said to follow him again, that was all. I have followed your instructions, nothing less and nothing more,' Arthur said.

'Come on, Arthur, please,' Harold said.

'He parked his car, got out and knocked at number four, and a frail-looking woman answered the door to him,' Arthur said.

'Enough of the monotone, boring description please. I know that's his mum,' Harold said. 'Go and knock. Use your initiative.'

'What? No way! That is not part of the deal,' Arthur said, having no intention of knocking or getting that close.

'If you don't then I'm going to tell your wife about you and the barmaid,' Harold said in his own monotone voice.

'I told you in confidence,' Arthur said. 'Anyway, nothing happened. There's nothing to tell.'

'I will tell her you took another woman's number and the guilt on your face will do the rest,' Harold said.

'Don't tell her – there's no need,' Arthur said. 'I'm getting out of the car now. I'll go and knock, I will, but what shall I say?'

'You'll think of something, if you know what's good for you,' Harold said.

Arthur put his phone back in his pocket and shut the car door he'd just opened. He sat still in his car. He didn't want to knock at the door. If he knocked and Jude clocked the blue car, he was old – what if Jude hit him? Or made a citizen's arrest? How would he explain any of this to his wife? Arthur jumped out of his skin – somebody was banging on his door. Should he run or open the door? He wanted to run.

'I know who you are, Arthur. Open the door – we need to speak to you,' the woman at the window said.

# CHAPTER THIRTY-THREE
## YOUNG JUDE

'How is this my fault exactly? Tell me,' Jude's dad said.

'If you'd just taken him to school like I'd asked then he wouldn't even be here, would he?' Jude's mum said.

'So, I should just leave you here? Is that it?' his dad said. 'God knows what you would do or what you'd take if I left you here alone.'

'You always have to bring that up, don't you,' his mum said. 'That was a one-off. A mistake, one time, and you always have to throw that in my face.'

'You could have died,' his dad said. 'I'm not the only one to keep bringing up one-off things from the past am I, honey?'

'Shhh, did you hear that?' his mum whispered, and put her hand in the air. 'I'm here, darling. Come and give me a cuddle. Everything's okay – mummy's here. Me and your dad have made up and we both love you very much,' his mum said more clearly.

Jude tried to stay still but his body jolted as he tried to stop sobbing. He knew that he'd called his mum earlier when he'd hurt himself but now that she was here, he didn't want to hear her patronising voice or see her smug face, the one that without saying one word would shout the words at him, 'Oh look what you've done, you silly boy'. He just wanted his mum and dad to go away.

'I told you to be quiet. Why do you have to drag your stupid clumpy shoes along the ground?' his mum said. 'You've scared him away now.'

'Me?' his dad said. 'He's not some rodent hiding from us.' Jude could hear the sarcasm in his dad's voice, even whilst he was hidden in the bushes. 'And if he has hidden himself away because we're too loud then it is you who started shouting for him, not me.'

'Ohh, be quiet,' his mum said again.

Jude could still hear them arguing in the distance. Neither of them was being quiet and they never were when they were together. He felt cold and was in pain, and didn't want to look at his arm but had to to see if it was okay, to see if he really did need his mum. He took his duffle coat off slowly and cautiously. He pulled his other arm out of his jumper first and then carefully rolled up the rest of it so he could pull it over his head and his injured arm all in one swift movement. There was a lot of blood; he had never seen so much before. He looked at the red sleeve of his T-shirt and gently pulled the last bit of it over his shoulder. He didn't want to look at what he'd done to his shoulder but, again, had to.

He braced himself and then looked at it as quickly as he could. There was a small hole in his shoulder – he retched. Blood was still slowly oozing out from the puncture wound. He had heard of a way at school, which he remembered from when they did some first-aid training, to stop or slow bleeding. He took his T-shirt off and then tied it tight above the wound on his shoulder and under his armpit. He then carefully draped his duffle coat back over his shoulders and held on to his jumper. He felt too much pain to try and put this back on as well. He could hear his parents walking back over towards him.

'If you had taken him to school and then came to find me, you could've done it that way around, no? Like a normal person,' his mum said.

'And then I would've left the boy worrying about you all day at school, and you have a nerve saying normal to me,' his dad said. 'Look, there is no easy answer. Except you need to stop doing this. The first time you did this, he was a baby – he couldn't remember. The next couple of times he would've been too young to remember as well, but now he's 10 years old and he'll remember this. You can't keep putting us through this. We need to move on.'

'Easy for you to say. How about me and my sister?' his mum said. They both immediately stopped in their tracks, as an all-encompassing sound screeched loudly like a wild animal would before it died. 'Mum, mum, help! Mum, help me!' Jude screamed, and then he passed out.

# CHAPTER THIRTY-FOUR
# HAROLD

The problem with reading or writing, Harold had always found, was once he'd started to read, or for that matter put pen to paper, he got into his rhythm and couldn't stop; he could be there for hours and in some cases days. The dust he'd always found unsettling, yet strangely comforting. He'd scrubbed at and cleaned the Book of Truth hundreds if not thousands of times, and the scriptures he'd done the same with. He used his hands, he used a duster, an old rag, he used cleaning products and he'd even tried shoe polish, but always to no avail.

Harold had read the first two scriptures and then started to read the third. The first scripture was about a gentleman named General William Day, he recalled. And the second told the story of a young man named Garner, who was travelling around the world. Whilst reading the scriptures, he felt like a detective trying to figure out the reasons for why these Utal divine occurrences had happened. He was never quite sure of why these people had been chosen – he could only guess – but he did have a strong inkling. He believed the reason why they were chosen was they were already doomed and were racing to their deaths. More specifically, these doomed souls were being given a chance of forgiveness for what they had already done wrong in their lives. One of these men was a killer, not by choice but still a killer nevertheless, and the second was a thief, a petty thief but all the same still a thief.

The third scripture was the Utal's promise. This was a short book containing a couple of promises. He would read one of them aloud daily, like a prayer, even when he'd hidden the books away. He knew this prayer off by heart.

He bowed his head. 'Forgiveness lies in the trust we show.'

'Are you still murmuring those old words, you fool,' the Utal said. 'I can forgive those who show me their trust. You took my words and twisted them. Your wife, I don't believe I requested you to – you know full well what you did.'

'You …' Harold began to say before backing down quickly.

'Read the fourth scripture, Harold, if you aren't too afraid, old man.'

'I'm not afraid …' Harold had begun to talk again, but the creature had disappeared.

Harold read the first word of the fourth scripture aloud: 'Harold'.

# CHAPTER THIRTY-FIVE
# ARTHUR

It was probably a neighbour asking him to not park in front of their house, Arthur was thinking rationally. Don't speed off – just wind the window down and say sorry and move on. He could see it was a woman so at least it wasn't Jude, he thought. He wound down his window and a mix of stale coffee and sweet perfume rushed into the car.

'Arthur Moreton, we know you have been following Jude Holmes – we know this is not the first time.'

'This is preposterous – who are you?' Arthur said. He hadn't seen this coming. He never expected her to be a police officer; she couldn't be. 'Show me some ID please?'

She showed him a professional-looking badge. Arthur was now convinced she was genuine, although he wasn't sure how he would tell if the badge was fake.

'PC Delia Kauffman,' she said. 'So now tell me what you're doing or we'll take this down to the station and we'll take a recorded statement. Your choice.'

'No, no, you can't take me down the station – I can't have my wife finding out about this,' Arthur said.

'About what?' the PC said. 'About Harold? About him

blackmailing you to follow Jude or about your secret?'

Arthur scrunched his eyes and hung his head in shame. 'All of what you just said, I guess.'

She leant in and touched Arthur on the shoulder. 'It's okay, Mr Moreton, I understand. What we're going to do is this.' She paused for effect and looked into the distance. 'I'm going to go back to my car – I'm in the unmarked silver BMW parked a few cars behind. You are going to follow me to Big Sam's coffee house around the corner and we are going to have a little chat about Harold. Do you understand me?'

'Yes, okay – thank you,' Arthur said, and immediately blushed afterwards. He wasn't sure why he'd said thank you.

'If you drive off, I will come to your house and arrest you in front of your wife,' the PC said. 'Neither of us want that to happen, do we?'

Arthur put his head in his hands. 'No, of course not,' he said.

'Bloody Harold,' he muttered. He waited for her to drive past and then indicated out.

# CHAPTER THIRTY-SIX
## YOUNG JUDE

Like all of his nights out with Ryan and his mates, things had started down the park with four or five bottles of lukewarm beer. Jude was wearing his best black trousers and his smartest burgundy Ted Baker shirt, and to top it off he had his black shined loafers on – he'd polished them the night before. He chugged on a Sovereign cigarette he'd promised to go twos on with Ryan, they walked to a cashpoint at their local supermarket and then they headed on the mission walk to The Sunken Ship. It took them close to half an hour to walk there and it was a cold night, but after a few beers Jude was pumped; he couldn't feel the cold.

'Has Tom texted you to say he'll meet us there?' Jude asked.

'Yes, mate – him and the usual crew are getting to the Ship for 9 or thereabouts,' Ryan said.

'Okay cool, mate. Hopefully we'll have a pint by then,' Jude said.

'Definitely – there's no reason why not. Tom said he'd been in the pub earlier today and the usual barmen are working tonight,' Ryan said. 'We'll get served easy.'

As they approached The Sunken Ship, they could see there were two heavy-looking doormen on the doors – not the usual scene; there were never bouncers on the doors. The pub was an old one and generally had oldies who stayed there the whole night, and then pretty much just Jude and his mates. Jude hesitated and looked at Ryan, who also looked nervous. As they reached the door, he felt the floor vibrate with the music.

'ID, lads,' the tallest chap said loudly.

The words they had dreaded. Jude and his mate fumbled looking in their pockets, knowing full well, and knowing the bouncers also knew, they would find no ID as there wasn't any. Not any ID that said that they were 18 anyway, because Jude and his friend were only 16.

'I had my passport on me, but I changed my trousers after spilling a beer. I must have left it behind,' Jude stuttered. 'Are you going in or coming with me, Ryan?'

'I'll come back to yours and we'll be back in half an hour. That okay, lads?' Ryan asked the doormen.

The doormen looked at each other and exchanged a smile and giggle. 'Go for it, lads,' the smaller doormen said.

Jude had turned and started to walk off. 'Guys, you're here. Come inside then,' the landlord said, whilst putting a cigarette in his mouth and lighting it up. He blew a puff of smoke out. 'Well, go in and warm up, lads.'

The doormen parted and Jude and Ryan walked through.

Jude smiled and laughed and gave Ryan a dig in the arm. 'The usual, mate?' Jude asked. 'I think I'll get us some shots as well. I think we deserve them after that, mate.'

'I'm not sure everyone else will get the same luck as us getting in,' Ryan said.

'True. I'll give Tom a bell to warn him,' Jude said.

Jude looked at his phone, just as he heard a familiar voice coming from behind him. 'Alright, boys!' Tom shouted. 'It's rocking in here tonight.'

'Yes, mate. This is going to be one hell of a night – I can already tell,' Jude said. 'Do you lot want some shots? Tom?'

'Not really, but you know me – I never say no to a drink,' Tom said. 'Get them in, lad, and I'll come and give you a hand when you've been served.

Jude looked down at his watch. The time had flown by; it was close to midnight. All the oldies had left at the usual closing time, half an hour or so ago. The pub was having a lockdown, and after putting back far too many drinks and confidently chatting to anyone who would engage with him, Jude had found out it was the landlord and his ex-wife's ironic twenty-year wedding anniversary. It turned out him and his wife had split ten years ago, but he wanted to celebrate what could have been rather than the day it really was – ten years divorced. Jude had seen the funny side and managed to piss the landlord off going on about how funny the landlord was.

He could see Tom was chatting to some girl and looked to be getting somewhere; on the other side of the table sat Ryan messing about playing Snake on his phone. Jude brought over two more pints and sat down, giving Ryan the other pint. Tom and the girl got up and went to sit at another table in the corner of the pub near the fireplace, and then they started kissing each other's faces off.

'Cheers, pal,' Ryan said.

'You looked a little bored sitting there, like a little loner,' Jude said, and laughed.

'I wasn't alone,' Ryan said. 'It was a little awkward, I'm not going to lie; I was trying to not listen too much to Tom's shameful chat-up lines.'

'You have to give it to him though – it seems to have worked well for him,' Jude said, as Ryan leant back in his chair and looked over at Tom and the girl groping each other.

'Fair play to him,' Ryan said.

Jude and Ryan stumbled out of The Sunken Ship an hour or so later.

'Sooooo,' Ryan's speech slurred.

'Sooooo what?' Jude mimicked Ryan, and laughed.

'You know, can I ask you a question? What happened with you and your parents?' Ryan asked.

Normally, Jude didn't talk about his family, but he'd drunk more than on a usual Friday night. 'I don't like them and they don't like me – that's about it,' Jude said, and laughed.

'Come on, I mean, I've never even heard you talk about your dad,' Ryan said. 'Sorry, I mean, is he alive?'

'Yes, yeah,' Jude said. 'Okay, I'll tell you a story. I'll tell you something I haven't shared with anyone.'

'Wow, man – that's deep,' Ryan said.

Jude laughed but was being deadly serious. 'When I was younger, I was about 10 years old,' Jude said, 'my mum went missing and me and my dad went to find her. My dad somehow knew she'd be at this abandoned castle. We go to the castle and surprise, surprise she is there. My dad goes to talk to her in this room in the castle and I'm left outside the room, and my dad tells me to wait there on my own. I'm not being funny but I was only little – I was shit scared on my own. I hear my mum say something about their wedding day and my dad with her sister. At the time, I didn't completely understand but I was upset about the whole situation and they were shouting at each other, so I ran off.'

'Mate, I was just asking to be polite. I don't need your life story,' Ryan said, and laughed again. But Jude knew he wanted to know more.

'Shall I continue? You did ask after all,' Jude said.

'No, go on. I am interested, really. It's like I am listening to a movie.'

'When I get outside the castle, I'm full of anger and I run at these rusty old castle doors to try and shut my parents inside. I hit the doors hard with my left shoulder,' Jude said and tapped his shoulder. 'I didn't see there was a protruding rusty nail in the door and I hit this with my shoulder. It goes in and out and I land back on the floor and scream in agony.'

'Ouch. Shit, man, that makes me feel a little sick,' Ryan said. 'I'm no good with gore. I can't even go for a blood test without nearly passing out.'

'Just you wait – you might need to sit down then,' Jude said.

'Nah, man, I'm fine – go on,' Ryan said.

'So, by the time my parents make it out of the castle, and they are still arguing, I've decided that actually my shoulder is not too bad and I go and hide from my parents,' Jude said. 'I'm annoyed with them still and I don't want to see them. I somehow make a tourniquet and stem the bleeding from my arm. I listen to my parents babbling on at each other. I look at my arm and retch. Time goes by and my parents walk off looking for me and shortly after, I hear them walking back. In this time, my adrenaline's worn off, but then my stomach starts to feel the worst pain I've felt in my life. I lift my shirt and the side of my stomach is bloated, and then when I inspect closer, I can see another wound on my side close to my hip but hardly any bleeding. I realise and panic the bleeding is on my insides. The world starts to go dizzy and I scream as loud as my lungs can.'

'Is this all true?' Ryan asked.

'Of course it is, Ryan,' Jude said.

'You know what? This has made me feel a little nauseous myself,' Ryan said.

'Shall I tell you the rest another time?' Jude asked.

'I think that's best,' Ryan said, and he ran quickly to the

bushes to throw up.

Jude knew it was more than likely because Ryan was so drunk, he wouldn't remember any of this conversation. That's what he hoped – he didn't want their friendship to change.

# CHAPTER THIRTY-SEVEN
## ARTHUR

The waiter had taken their orders. Arthur sat opposite to PC Delia Kauffman and her partner. He hadn't bothered to learn her partner's name, and actually wasn't sure if it had even been mentioned – he didn't care either. He couldn't concentrate; he wanted to get up and drive home to his wife.

'It's important you don't lie to us, Arthur,' the PC said. 'Am I making myself clear? This is going to go one of two ways. One, we talk and you give me all the details you know about Harold. Or two, you lie to me and deny what you know. I think we know this will lead to a cell for the night and who knows how many more nights in jail.'

'I've got two Americanos and one latte with coconut milk,' the waitress said. 'Who ordered the latte?'

'Yes, me,' Arthur said. 'Thank you.' The waitress put all the drinks down on the table and left them to it. He knew he was being paranoid but felt like the waitress knew; she knew he was being questioned by the police. And what if she knows someone who knows my wife? He knew he was being paranoid but couldn't help it. There were a million scenarios running through his head and none of the outcomes had good endings.

The PC took a big slurp of her coffee before she started with her questions. Her mannerisms and everything she did irritated Arthur; he felt himself getting more and more annoyed the longer he sat with her. Arthur answered all her questions honestly. He told her how he'd met Harold after his dad had died in the war, how they had been pen pals and how they had kept in touch all these years. And how he'd mistakenly thought he could confide in Harold.

'Sergeant, any questions you would like to ask?' the PC asked her partner.

'Arthur, what do you know about the cult?' the sergeant asked. 'Are you in Harold's cult? Are you a member or are you one of the leaders?'

'Arthur dropped his drink in shock. He hurriedly grabbed some napkins before his drink spilt on to the two police officers' laps. 'I'm, I don't know. I haven't, he isn't part of a cult, is he?'

'Remember what I said about lying and where this will end if you lie to us,' the PC said.

'I'm not lying though,' Arthur said. 'I've answered everything I know, honestly I have.'

'The book – you must have read the cult book?' the sergeant asked.

'What book? What are you talking about?' Arthur said.

'Elizabeth Beecham and her son Todd and Harold's wife – what do these people mean to you? the PC asked.

'His wife died a long time ago, I know that. He said his wife had died, that's all I know,' Arthur said. 'And I don't know an Elizabeth or her son.'

'The Utal? The creature?' she asked.

'The what?' Arthur said. He felt bombarded and confused; the questions didn't make any sense.

'You really are just his little errand boy, aren't you?' The sergeant said. He scratched the stubble on his chin, adjusted his collar and shook his head. 'We're done here, PC Kaufman. Let's go.'

Arthur sat on his own; he was relieved the police officers had believed him, but offended they thought he was Harold's little errand boy. He then realised they had stitched him up and left without paying for their drinks. Arthur was so relieved they'd gone, he didn't mind paying for their drinks. He looked around and tried to catch the waiter's attention.

# CHAPTER THIRTY-EIGHT
# HAROLD

He wiped his brow, adjusted his reading glasses and reopened the fourth scripture. Harold had started to read this many years ago. But he knew then like he did now, if he was to read until the end of the book, he would find out about his own fate. Death had never worried him before, but as he'd got older and his end was nearing, he feared it more than ever.

He turned over the front cover and on to the first page, which described his sins and why these were the reasons for his selection to be reborn. Number one: going to war. Harold never felt this was a sin but knew better than to question the Utal. The next part Harold agreed wholeheartedly with and he was ashamed to this day. He'd frozen; he couldn't move – bullets kept firing in his direction. He'd been told to be the checker, that was his job, his only job; it was supposed to be a simple job. The war was over and everyone knew it, and he'd done this job many times before without any problems. But when he'd seen so many Nazis were coming his way, he'd frozen and lost the ability to speak, to shout to warn his friends, his comrades.

He somehow hadn't been spotted by the Nazis. Maybe it was because he couldn't move, he was so still, he looked dead or they didn't realise he was there. The scripture described him as a coward who left his comrades to die when serving in the war, and how he had the audacity to later take credit and be awarded a medal for bravery for his efforts in that particular battle. This in turn had helped him get a job some years after the war in a secret government role. He was the ultimate coward pocketing money from his sins. The last time he had read some of this scripture, his wife Barbara wasn't included and now she was. He skipped this part and moved on to the last page.

*Forgiveness lies in the trust we show,* the last page began, *but trust can be misplaced.* Harold was chosen in between the hundred-year sequence. His birthday was 25th April, the date of General William and young Garner's deaths, the date of all past divine occurrences. Harold was one of many people born on this date but he had more sins than everyone else. He was chosen because the world needed a sacrifice more regularly, as people killed the planet they lived on. For all his sins he had been chosen to save the world for now, with one sacrifice, and for this he'd be given his choice of reincarnation, eternal life or forgiveness.

He knew forgiveness was all he wanted, his wife's forgiveness. The last line read: the old mind is wiser than the young, but the young mind sees what the old mind has already forgotten.

Harold didn't understand the last line at all. He knew Lewis would be a risk but he could surely trust him? This was his last chance to atone for his sins and he didn't have any choice or anyone else to help him make the sacrifice. Lewis will have to do, Harold thought. He didn't have time to change his plans.

# CHAPTER THIRTY-NINE
# YOUNG JUDE

The room was almost pitch black, except for a slit in the blinds that was letting some light in infrequently as cars drove past. After the initial panic Jude had felt once he'd realised that he wasn't in his own bed, he'd worked out all the tubes attached to him and his veins were for his own benefit; he had calmed down a little bit. He thought these tubes must be working as he couldn't feel any pain; saying that, he couldn't feel much altogether. His eyes were tired and he was adjusting to the limited light. He'd worked out the snoring he was hearing was in fact coming from his mum sitting on the chair next to his bed – he wasn't alone. He settled and started to drift back to sleep.

'Hello, dear,' his mum said softly, as she rubbed his arm tentatively. 'Are you awake now, my dear? How are you feeling today? My poor little solider.'

He had been awake on and off for a few hours; his mum's pig-like snoring hadn't helped matters. He was also now in quite a bit of pain. 'No, my stomach is really sore. Take the pain away please, mum,' he moaned.

'Nurse, come quickly!' his mum shouted out.

'It's okay, mum – it's just a little sore, that's all,' Jude said. He stopped moaning and tried to reassure her that he was okay.

'If you go and jump into sharp nails on a door then that's what happens, dear,' his mum said in a matter-of-fact tone. 'You've had me worried sick about you. They had to operate; you had internal bleeding. You are lucky to be alive. But I guess the main thing is you are on the mend now. The nurse will give you some more morphine soon and it will make you feel lots better, for now.'

The nurse came in, smiled and adjusted his medication quickly. She then left him with his mum, alone together again. Even the nurse looked like she was trying to avoid his mum, Jude thought.

He turned his head away from his mum. His body was too sore to turn over, but he was already annoyed with her again and didn't want her to see him cry. 'I need some more sleep,' he said.

Days turned into weeks and weeks turned into months. Jude was still in hospital. Not once had his mum mentioned the real reason for him being stuck in the hospital; not once did she say sorry to him.

'Mum, what happened with Dad and your sister?' Jude asked.

'Ohh, my dear – I'm not sure this conversation is appropriate for your little ears, sweetheart,' she said.

She would always try her best to avoid difficult situations. Jude knew she would speak to him like this, with her passive-aggressive mumsy charm that was unique to only her.

'I know more than you think, Mum,' Jude said. 'I'm not a child, well, technically I am, but it doesn't mean I don't know what adults do. Did he and my auntie sleep together. On your wedding night, Mum?'

'Well, darling, like father like son. You should wash your

mouth out with soap – like all males, they all know about sex and that is the only thing they know,' his mum said. She looked away avoiding his eye contact. 'That's the only thing men care about.'

Jude batted away her insults like flies. 'Did they, Mum?' he said, determined to get an answer.

'Yes, yes,' his mum said. 'You have to push me and push me, don't you.'

Jude didn't know what to say to console his mum. He could see she was upset but he'd lived most of his life with her crying for no reason. At least he now knew there was a reason. He watched as she tried to stop the floods of tears.

'Are you happy now?' his mum asked. 'You've made your own mum cry.'

'Happy?' Jude said, and laughed a nervous laugh.

'You know you're the only reason I continue with this miserable existence,' his mum said. 'If I wasn't already pregnant when they, well, you know, the little know-it-all that you are. Well, I could have killed myself right at that moment when I saw them in bed together. That would have taught them a lesson. And I would have gladly, but I couldn't, because of you, dear. That is the only reason.'

Jude knew his mum was malicious and knew how her tongue had hurt so many friends and family they never saw anymore; but this was the worst, this was the lowest she had sunk. He felt more hurt and angry than he'd ever felt.

# CHAPTER FOURTY
## ARTHUR

Arthur was talking to himself as he did from time to time, especially when he felt aggrieved. 'Why should he get away with it? He's spent his whole life getting away with it. He has got away with it for far too long, but not anymore.'

'Would you like another drink, Sir?' the waiter asked as she picked up the mugs and cleared the table.

Arthur looked a little startled, but he was back in the room. He felt embarrassed and his face had reddened; he'd clearly been talking to himself when she came over.

'Sorry to give you a fright. I'm always chatting to myself as well – don't you worry,' she proudly said.

'I was in my own world – my apologies,' Arthur said.

'Coffee, Sir?' she asked.

'No, thanks – just the bill. I better get going,' Arthur said quietly. He was self-conscious he'd been chatting to himself, but mainly he felt paranoid that not just the waiter but also everyone else in the place knew what had just happened with the police. He was a criminal in everyone's eyes in the café, he was sure of it. He paid the bill sharply and kept his head down as he made his way out to his car. He definitely wouldn't be drinking there again.

Arthur knew the truth about his dad. He knew why Harold had come to tell him and his grandparents about the death of his father, all those years ago. He wasn't stupid and hated that Harold thought he was. He knew it was guilt, but for a long time Harold had been caring and interested in Arthur and his life. He was happy to ironically have a father figure to talk to. His grandad was there but he didn't ask about his day or show much interest in him, right up until he and his grandmother died within a short space of time of each other in the fifties – they just did the minimum. Arthur was forever grateful they hadn't sent him away to a home for orphans; at the time, that would have been an easy option for them and he was forever worrying that was what would happen. They would often tell him that they didn't bring him into this world but they did their best to feed him and put a roof over his head.

There had never been the right time to talk to Harold. As time went on, Arthur could never find the moment and he didn't know how to bring it up – too much time had passed. But as Harold grew older, he changed; he wasn't the same person who would look out for him, be it through guilt or a genuine care for his welfare. He'd turned into a manipulative, nasty piece of work. He hadn't lived close enough to Harold to know the ins and outs of how he and his wife lived, but one day they were chatting on the phone and Harold had just mentioned his wife had died, like he was talking about a character off a sitcom. It had felt as if it meant nothing to him.

He'd never read the book the police mentioned, but Harold had talked to him about the Book of Truth and about some other nonsense – he'd spoken in riddles. He'd mentioned the Utal on one phone call but only that once, but at the time, Arthur thought Harold was just being odd or he was quoting a programme off TV and trying to fool him somehow. Arthur was often the butt of a practical joke that Harold would play. But it was never mentioned again and he hadn't thought about it until the police had just brought it up.

His phone started to ring – it was Harold again. 'Arthur, what are you doing? Did you scare Jude?' he asked.

'Yes,' Arthur said. 'I did what you said.'

Arthur hung up his phone and headed for his car. He was going to pay Harold a little visit.

# CHAPTER FORTY-ONE
# THE WRITER

The writer had spent the whole day contemplating whether to write a new letter or not, but had decided to pop out instead. The writing was a therapeutic way of letting off some steam; literally, this is what their therapist had told them. Most days the writer took their advice, but not today.

The front window had been left open and there were no lights on; good job I'm not a thief, the writer thought. I'm much worse than that.

After gently tiptoeing around the house and making sure Harold definitely wasn't in, the writer saw it near the front door, the post that had just been left on the side unit in the hallway. Their hard work had been discarded. Mind you, this was just one of a pile of many unopened envelopes left to gather dust. The writer opened the envelope and made sure it was their work and it was still correct – it hadn't been tampered with. Then they headed upstairs and glued the letter to a large mirror above the sink in the bathroom.

'Perfect, well almost,' the writer said. 'I won't be ignored.'

With a red lipstick, the writer wrote a new message in capitals at the top of the mirror, right above the letter they had just glued to the mirror.

# CHAPTER FORTY-TWO
## JUDE
## PRESENT DAY

Jude was embarrassed but he had to make the call; he couldn't continue like this. It was no way to live. He'd spent last night sleeping in his car again; he had thought about asking to sleep at his mum's in his old bedroom but thought better of it. Apart from it being no way to live, sleeping in his car was terribly uncomfortable – his body ached all over and he felt rigid. He opened the driver's door, stumbled out of his car and stretched and yawned. He then fumbled around in his pocket and looked for his phone; he jumped as he heard it start to ring. It was ringing but the sound wasn't coming from his pockets, but from the car. He found the phone just in time before it rang out, but then saw it was his mum calling him and decided against answering it. He looked for Nigel in his contacts list and called his number.

'Hi mate – how are you?' Nigel said – he'd picked up after one ring. 'I was honestly just about to call you.'

'Yeah, yeah, no need to be polite,' Jude said.

'I really was – I heard you had lost your job. And guess what – I have a job for you, if you'd like to work with me again that is?' Nigel asked.

'Really?' Jude was amazed. 'Are you being serious?'

'Sure. The position isn't for *Man Issues* though. We are going on air. I thought you have the perfect, well, face for radio,' Nigel joked.

Jude laughed. He always loved working with Nigel; they both had a silly sense of humour, and he really needed to laugh. He laughed and laughed – tears rolled down his face, until he began to cry.

'Hey, man. If you don't want the job, just say, man. It's not that bad – no need to cry about it,' Nigel said.

Jude laughed again, and concentrated on gaining back his composure. He was making awkward sob sounds and was embarrassed. He'd had a tough time since losing his job and his mum had never been the type of mum to give him a shoulder to cry on. The tears had to come out at some point. He'd surprised himself by crying, especially on the phone to Nigel. He'd never live this down, but at least he hadn't cried in front of his mum.

'Thanks, Nigel. You are a true gentleman,' Jude said. 'You really are.'

'Is that a yes, you'll take the job I hear?' Nigel asked.

'Of course, mate – thank you,' Jude said.

'Great,' Nigel said. 'It's a 6am start and you start tomorrow.'

'Hey, that's early and tomorrow? What, are you sure?' Jude asked. 'What would you have done if I'd said no?'

'I would've hosted it, but you know me. My face is more suited to the TV,' Nigel said.

They both laughed, but there was no crying this time around.

# CHAPTER FOURTY-THREE
# HAROLD

Harold heard a scream and jumped up out of his seat. 'Is everything all okay up there, Jane?' he called out.

'I think you need to come and see this,' Jane shouted down to Harold.

Harold made his way upstairs and as he did, he could see Jane looking at something in the bathroom mirror.

'What is it?' Harold asked, but before she answered he could already see.

He read the writing that was in red lipstick first: 'Do you still believe in this nonsense? Your dead wife, Barb,' Harold quietly said. He didn't even read the letter attached below. 'Was this you? Did you write this?'

'Me?' Jane said, looking shocked. 'Shall I call the police? They can find out who did this. They can find out anything these days.'

'I think you should go,' Harold said loudly. He pushed past her, grabbed a towel off the rails, wiped the lipstick off the mirror and then threw the dirty towel in the bath.

'I haven't finished cleaning yet and anyway, I'm not sure if it's safe to leave you here alone. What if they come back?'

Jane said. 'I can stay over for the night. I can stay until the police find out who did this.'

'No,' Harold said. 'You can't – you have Lewis to take care of.'

'He can stay too – the more the better I reckon,' Jane said.

'No, I've already said no and that is final,' Harold said. 'I have looked after myself all these years and I've been okay up until now. And we are not calling the police – I won't hear anything more about it.'

Jane didn't look best pleased. 'A cup of tea then?' she asked. 'Something to calm yours and my nerves.'

Harold sipped his tea; it was just how he liked it. He mainly drunk coffee as it had more of a bitter kick which he liked, but Jane knew how to make a lovely brew. He sat at his wooden table in the kitchen and watched her as she busied herself.

'Well,' Jane said, as she wiped down the sides with a piping-hot dishcloth.

'Well, what?' Harold said.

'What is all that about?' Jane asked.

'Some crazy person pretending to be my late wife?' Harold asked. 'How should I know?'

'No,' Jane said, 'well, yes, that as well, but the letter below it, about a sacrifice and a Ute or something, and it was about you being a constant or something. Was it about you? I don't know.'

'A Utal,' Harold said. 'I think it said a Utal. Anyway, I know about as much as you do. It's a load of nonsense like my wife said,' Harold said, and laughed.

Jane wasn't laughing, and she continued to clean the kitchen. 'It sounds like the funny things you used to write about when I was little. Anyway, my boy mentioned last night he's coming over to see you tonight. I'll send him straight over when I see him, once he's finished school,' she said. 'I know you don't want to hear this, but don't immediately say no. Have a think about calling the police for me, please.'

Harold mumbled something; Jane couldn't understand him so she continued.

'Forget about the scary message for a moment,' she said. 'Someone has broken into your house. You don't go out much, so you were probably in the house when they broke in. Like I said, don't say anything now – I don't expect you to – just have a think. I'm thinking of your safety.'

'Okay,' Harold mumbled – this time it was a word Jane could hear and understand.

'Good, right, you have my number,' Jane said. 'My mobile is on loud. I'll answer anytime – call me if you need me. Don't be afraid to call.'

'I appreciate it, I really do,' Harold said. 'Are you sure you still want Lewis coming over here? Do you think he'll be safe?'

'Lewis, he'll be fine – trust me,' Jane said, and gave Harold a kiss on the cheek, as she picked up her bits ready to leave and made her way to the door. 'And next time I see you – I haven't forgotten – I expect an apology.' The door slammed shut.

'Sorry,' Harold said, too late for her to hear him.

# CHAPTER FOURTY-FOUR
# HAROLD
# THREE DAYS BEFORE

After an eventful morning, Harold hummed and hawed for the rest of the day. He hadn't eaten much all day and struggled to keep down an egg mayonnaise sandwich; it gave him instant heartburn, and he had washed it down with a scorching-hot coffee which only made matters worse. He was unsure if he should tell Lewis about the book – what if he then told his mum? But he had a plan and this was his chance. The scriptures and the Utal had been clear; if he was to make amends and gain the Utal's trust and, most importantly, his wife's forgiveness, he must stick to the plan – this was his last chance.

He looked across the kitchen table. Lewis looked amused and pushed the book back towards Harold.

'What do you think of the book?' Harold asked.

Lewis didn't talk for a moment; Harold let the question hang in the air.

'This is your religion. Am I right?' Lewis asked. 'Are you part of some weird cult or something?'

'This is the Book of Truth,' Harold said. 'It is not my

religion and it's definitely not some cult. A long time ago I was chosen and last night you were chosen to guide me. Do you understand?' Harold asked.

'Guide you? Are you okay? Do you need me to call someone? Like a doctor?' Lewis said sarcastically, and shook his head. 'That recent bump on your head did some real damage. This book doesn't say anything about me or about me being your guide. It doesn't say much at all to be honest.'

'It will,' Harold tried to assure Lewis. 'Anyway, all you have to do is bring Jay to me. Next time you play footy, he can jump over the fence to get the ball.'

'Do you want him to be the sacrifice?' Lewis asked. 'That's what the couple of lines in the book say. They say about a sacrifice.'

'No. I'm old, but I'm not crazy,' Harold said firmly.

'What do you want from him then and what is this book all about?' Lewis asked.

'One, your mum said Jay is the one you've been fighting with – would you like to scare him?' Harold lied, but he thought Lewis might see this as a good prank to play on his friend.

'Yeah, okay – it might be a laugh. But the book?' Lewis asked.

'You didn't let me finish. Two, the book is part of the trick,' Harold said. He'd decided to go with a different tactic.

'But you were saying about us being chosen,' Lewis said.

'I was getting into my character. Trust me, we can really scare him – no more fights. You want to play a trick on Jay or not?' Harold asked.

Harold knew he was taking a gamble with Lewis and that he had no chance of getting him to believe or to follow, but surely if he could still find a sacrifice, that would be enough to save the world, to save himself, to be forgiven, he hoped.

'Go on then – it sounds a laugh,' Lewis said. 'It'll be a few nights away though. Jay's been off sick from school the last few days. I can't see him coming to play football for a while – he has a real bad gut. The proper runs.'

'I see. That's okay – just let me know in advance before you both come over,' Harold said.

'You know you're weird though, right?' Lewis said.

'Of course – is there any fun to be had being normal? Harold asked.

'I guess not,' Lewis said, and left for home. 'I'll see you in a few days.

Shortly after Lewis had gone, Harold sat down on his sofa and made himself comfortable, and the Utal sat down next to him.

# CHAPTER FOURTY-FIVE
## JUDE
## PRESENT DAY

His home smelt unfamiliar; a trail of stale old dog lingered in the air. Jude opened some windows, sprayed a couple of puffs of lemon and lime air freshener around the house and made himself a fresh coffee. This surely would make the place smell a little better or at least mask it. He loved the aroma of freshly brewed coffee and was parched. Although he desperately missed Dylan, he hadn't had a chance to pick him up from Ryan's yet, but he'd thought about it and decided against it for now. Ryan didn't know he was back yet and he could do with the time to set up for tomorrow morning. And, more importantly, he didn't feel safe himself yet; he didn't want to put Dylan at risk again.

Jude typed Nigel's name into his phone and pressed dial.

'Hi, Jude. Have you had a chance to think of anything specific or any topics you'd like to add to your slot tomorrow?' Nigel asked.

'Depends on how risk-averse you are,' Jude said. 'I wouldn't want to shut your new show down within one day of being on air.'

'Okay, right, I have everything written up,' Nigel said. 'You could go with what I've done already. I would prefer you didn't get us thrown off air within our first two-hour slot, to be honest. Have you read my script I sent over?' Nigel asked.

'Yes, it looks good. How about the bit where you have the local news, the good and the bad? It's short. I'll keep your good, if we can take my bad?' Jude suggested.

'The good and the bad literally takes up five minutes – how much damage can you do in five minutes?' Nigel said. 'Saying that, how many people will be listening to us at 6am, and how many people will even be listening to our new radio show?'

'You must have some projections, no?' Jude said.

'I was just trying to make you feel better, in case you muck it up. I don't want to make you more nervous by saying about *Man Issues'* massive following tuning in for our first *People Issues* radio show,' Nigel said. 'To be honest, it's your honesty our listeners will want to hear – this is why I asked you to host the show. When you left, so did a lot of our readers. We started the magazine together; it's only fair we can share some success together. I know you've been hard done by the *Gazette* – if you want to have a dig at them, then go for it.'

'I appreciate your loyalty, I do. And it would be fair to say the same can't be said for me, when …' Jude started to say.

'Don't be silly. I understood at the time that you left to better your career and that's fine. You've been unfortunate and now you're lucky because this radio show will put you back on course, in the spotlight,' Nigel said.

'The thing is, the *Gazette*, it's not just a dig …' Jude tried to finish his sentence again, but Nigel interrupted. 'You say your piece, I understand. Tomorrow, we'll be a hit, you mark my words. Anyway, you need some beauty sleep. Go on –

night, pal.' Nigel put the phone down before Jude could say another word.

Jude looked at his phone and muttered to himself, 'I'll definitely be in the spotlight, that's for sure.' Then a text from his mum lit up; he was told it was urgent and he must come round at once. He grabbed his coat and keys and headed over to his mum's.

# CHAPTER FORTY-SIX
## TIFF

The sweats in the middle of the night, the shivers, the uncontrollable shakes and screams had tormented Tiff ever since that night. She had never had a good night's sleep since the night she was almost killed by her own mum and Harold. She remembered everything, every last detail, even though every day she tried her hardest to forget.

On her way in, she had second thoughts. She went back outside and stood and leant against the brick wall next to the entrance doors. She puffed on two cigarettes, one straight after another, her red lipstick staining each one. She took a few deep breaths and walked confidently back into Livewell care home. She had planned her visit; the receptionist, although she looked surprised, did know Tiff was coming here to see her mum. The receptionist had a strange beetroot-like complexion and after her initial look of confusion, she then mumbled on and on until the words hit Tiff like a punch to the gut: 'She might not have long left – she has taken a turn for the worse,' she said. Tiff asked if they were talking about the same person, but they were. And although she hated her mum to the very core, she was upset;

she didn't want to be – she hated that she was upset – but she was.

She headed back outside and smoked another two cigarettes. She needed them – she felt oddly dizzy and needed to compose herself. A few minutes later, she walked back inside the care home and waited for someone to escort her to her mum. As she walked down the bleached corridors, she ate a couple of mints to take the old ashtray taste out of her mouth. She walked into her mum's room. She didn't know what to expect – the room smelt like old people, must, disinfectant and cats, but most of all it smelt like death.

'The rumours are true then,' Elizabeth laughed, a laugh which turned into the sound of a witch's cackle, sending shivers down her daughter's spine. She proceeded to have a coughing fit and a carer had to come in and sit her upright, placing a few pillows behind her to support her back. The carer gave her a glass of water and she took a couple of sips. The carer warned Tiff to not get her too excited and left them alone again.

They sat in silence for a while, looking each other up and down, taking in how different they both now looked.

'You look like death,' Tiff said bluntly.

'It comes to us all,' Elizabeth said. 'You look different too. Did I do this to you? Is this my fault?' she asked.

'Do you mean that I'm not your Todd anymore?' Tiff asked. 'Our bond was well and truly gone a long time ago; you definitely killed that. Is that what you're asking?'

'Wait a minute,' Elizabeth said, and held her hand up.

'No, you wait a minute – you'll have your turn, not that you deserve one,' Tiff said. 'Let me tell you, there are many things that are most definitely your fault. But this, me being me, no, you're not taking any credit for this. I'm Tiff and I'm proud – this is the one and only aspect of my life that I'm proud of. So, no, you most definitely had nothing to do with it. And you will not take any credit.'

'Tiff – that isn't even a real name,' Elizabeth smirked.

'You really are a piece of shit, aren't you,' Tiff said. 'You haven't even asked how I am. Or if I've somehow recovered from the hell that you put me through.' She was trying not to get angry – her mum wasn't worth it – but it was so difficult to keep her temper.

The room fell silent again.

'You know, I've tried to contact you many times. I've ...' Elizabeth tried to say, and then she stopped. 'I'm sorry, I am ...' Elizabeth wiped tears away from her eyes.

'Don't give me those crocodile tears,' said Tiff. 'As you know, I had a visitor that you sent my way. He wanted me to give my version of events – my version! Can you believe it? He said it in those words, as if there is more than one version of what happened on that night.'

Elizabeth let out a strangulated sob-like sound and continued to wipe tears away from her face.

'I remember – I will never forget,' Tiff said. 'You and that weird son of a bitch tried to kill me. And I remember a woman called Barb. She hit him and you suddenly had a change of heart about killing me. I remember all of that.'

'That's right,' Elizabeth said. 'I didn't go through with it. I untied your restraints. I got you up ...'

'You were talked around because you'd been caught,' Tiff said. 'And then, yes, you did take my restraints off, the restraints you tied me down with. You took the gag out of my mouth and helped me to be sick to get the drugs out of me, the drugs you had forced down me, to try and kill me with. You only let me go because you were caught. You're sorry because you were caught. Let me ask you this: how sorry are you about killing Barb?'

Elizabeth's face changed: she looked shocked.

'I know. I sat outside in our car, like you had told me to,'

Tiff said. 'And I sat there for what seemed a lifetime and I waited and I waited. You weren't coming back out of the house and you definitely weren't coming back for me. And then I heard the scream – I will never forget that scream, the blood-curdling cry. I feel guilty that I didn't go back to help her. She had saved me and then I had left her with you and him; but I was a child – what could I do? You, on the other hand, how do you feel? Is it the guilt that is finally killing you?'

'Time has passed. But of course I feel guilty – I'm not a monster,' Elizabeth said.

There was a pause in conversation. Tiff walked away from her mum and shook her head.

'You're not a monster? You do make me laugh,' Tiff said. 'I mean, in some kind of twisted way it's funny that you actually think you're not a monster. What kind of person kills another living human being and thinks they're not a monster? What kind of person? A parent who has tried to kill their own child and they think that's normal? It's psychotic. You are the biggest monster that has ever lived, that is what you are. When you finally die, and God that can't come soon enough, as you're dying, remember that is exactly what you are – a monster.'

Elizabeth bit her lip and looked aimlessly out of the window; she tugged at her duvet. 'You know, I was a victim as well. I had been brainwashed,' she said.

'Pull the other one. Can you not take any responsibility in your sordid little life, or are you just going to pass the buck until your final breath?' Tiff said, and clenched her fists, still holding back her temper the best she could.

'What can I do? How can I make amends? I'll do anything you say,' Elizabeth said.

'For a start, you need to go to the nearest police station and hand yourself in. You need to admit your crimes; you've

lived a free life and you may be dying or you might not be –
I don't actually care,' Tiff said. 'But if you have any remorse
or if you've ever loved me, you'll go to the police station or
you'll get them to come here if need be, that is if you are
truly too weak and feeble to leave this bed. After this, you'll
spend whatever time you have left behind bars. Because that
is what you deserve.'

'Do you not care that I'm dying? Elizabeth asked.

'No, I don't,' Tiff said. 'Know this: if I'd come back into
that house in a vain attempt to save Barb, I know you and
your weird accomplice would have killed me as well. And
you know this is true.'

The room fell silent for the last time. Elizabeth didn't say
a word and Tiff didn't break the silence and didn't wait to
hear what Elizabeth had to say. She only hoped for once in
her life her mum would do what was right. She looked back
at her mum for what could be the last time and then left. She
didn't shed one tear as she left that horrid care home.

# CHAPTER FORTY-SEVEN
# HAROLD
# TWO DAYS BEFORE

The Utal spat the words out aloud and Harold jotted everything it said down on to a notepad. Later, he would write his notes up neatly on to the next page of the Book of Truth.

Harold took a moment to get up and pour a glass of juice, and proceeded to wash down his medicine with it. And after half an hour, the blurred vision he'd suffered earlier had disappeared and he could see clearly again. He could hear and see the Utal clearer than ever and with that, it was gone.

For Harold, everything made more sense. He pricked his finger and squeezed it as he wrote the notes into the Book of Truth with his own blood. The book lifted up into the air and then smashed back down violently to the ground. The Utal appeared again – it crawled up on to Harold and sat on the bridge of his nose.

'I trust this time you won't let me down,' the Utal said. 'I have chosen the young. I don't want a different and older sacrifice – I won't accept it this time around. If you're unsuccessful, not only will you suffer, the world will too and feel the consequences of your failure. Everyone will feel my raft.'

Like a magician, the Utal vanished. Harold was tired. He slowly climbed the staircase, moaning after every step. He walked into his room, curled up in the foetal position under his duvet on his bed and fell in and out of sleep.

'You'll pay for what you did to me,' he could hear Barb say again and again. He rubbed his ears and tried to stop hearing her. She was dead; he couldn't hear her – she's not real, he told himself.

He snapped himself awake and sat bolt upright. He remembered the anger he'd felt when his own wife had hit him and she was the reason the sacrifice had escaped. Barb was the only option; there had to be a sacrifice. He'd had no choice but to kill her. He couldn't kill Elizabeth – she was meant to be the follower, the believer.

He remembered Barb and her innocent, pleading face as he restrained her. Elizabeth was no help; the only help she gave was when they buried his wife. And more than that, her silence, but Harold now knew this came from a selfish place. If she was a true follower, a true believer, then she would have brought back her son, the world would have been saved and the Utal would leave him be, he thought.

# CHAPTER FOURTY-EIGHT
## HAROLD
## ON THE DAY
## PART ONE

Harold paced up and down in his garden; he was leaving a muddy track behind him with each lap he walked. He'd decided he needed more medicine – his meds weren't working the way they should, the way they used to. He was weak, his mind was weak and he needed too much sleep; he needed to up his dose. He took four tablets in the morning and wasn't hungry, so he skipped breakfast and just had a coffee.

He went back into his kitchen and poured himself another hot coffee; he was feeling drained again. The second hand ticked, ticked, ticked and then stopped. He had been sitting in his kitchen looking at the French-themed, oversized clock on the wall. Until time had completely stopped that is. He got up to take a closer look, took the clock off the wall and held it up to his ear. He could hear the tick; he put the clock back on the wall. He sat back down and looked up at the clock: tick, tick, tick. He fidgeted with his fingernails and again stared at the clock watching as time ticked by.

The time was now approaching early evening; this was the time Lewis said he and Jay would play football. Lewis and Jay still hadn't arrived and Harold hadn't seen the Utal all day. He needed the Utal's instructions; he felt nervous. Time had stopped again. He got up and walked towards the clock, but before he reached it, he heard the familiar voice.

'Time waits for no man, Harold,' the Utal said to him.

Harold had heard that famous phrase before, but he couldn't recall where.

'Time has stopped and it will stand still until the sacrifice has been made,' the Utal said. With that, it disappeared and Harold continued to sit and look at the clock as time stood still.

Harold muttered the words to himself, 'The world is in my hands.'

# CHAPTER FOURTY-NINE
# HAROLD

The kitchen walls started to close in. Harold moved to the back door but what he saw was far from what he expected: a raging scarlet red fire. He found as many tea towels as he could muster and lay them at the bottom of the door to cover the seal – he had to stop the smoke from coming in. He inhaled the smoke that had already seeped through. His chest felt tight; he covered his mouth and started to cough. He needed water to drink but had no time; the walls were getting closer. He looked over to the front door, which was open, and walked towards it.

'Help!' Harold's panicked voice shouted. He kept walking and walking but was getting no closer to the front door. The floor felt like a treadmill; he could walk and run but was going nowhere – there was no escape.

'Keep going, Harold,' the Utal said mockingly. Harold looked around the room but couldn't see it. 'I'm omnipresent, Harold. You don't have to see me to be able to hear or talk to me – you should know this by now. I'm always listening, watching and waiting.'

Harold closed his eyes, covered his ears and ran; his legs

felt springy and athletic like he was 20 again. He ran as fast as he could, but he was going nowhere.

'Running with your eyes shut is probably not a wise idea, especially not at your ripe old age,' the Utal said.

Harold pressed his hands over his ears tighter and ran harder and faster. 'You can't control me, you can't control me,' Harold repeated, as he ran. He came to an abrupt stop and opened his eyes. He felt prickly grass on his skin – he was lying on the lawn in his back garden. A man covered in muck and dripping wet, in full old-fashioned army attire, stood over him.

'Get up, man – don't let the other lads down,' General William Day said. 'We need to go before they catch us.' He looked at the General as he stretched out his hand to be helped to his feet. How could he be here? He's dead and within the scriptures, he was young and now he's old – how?

'No time to stop; time is everything. Time is all you have,' the General said.

Yes, time – that's it. Harold took his hand and stood up. He could see four faces in the distance but they were getting closer. One of them was Lewis – he could tell it was him by his hair and his scruffy clothes – but he was walking backwards. Arthur, with eyes small and like daggers, stood completely still and staring; his eyes seemed to be able to see right through him. Harold looked at his chest and he had two holes going through his torso – no blood. He looked back at Arthur who was still completely static, but now he was standing in front of him in his garden. In the distance there was a boy who looked like Jay. He had blood all over his top and his face was red with blood, part of it caved in. 'You did this,' the boy who looked like Jay said. And, lastly, a man with no face stood with his phone taking photos. Behind the four men, he could see two women and a little boy and girl. They looked happy. He squinted until he could finally just make out Elizabeth and Barb. Barb was back – she was alive.

'Barb, it's me, Harold,' Harold shouted. 'I'm sorry for what I did to you – the Utal made me do it.' Barb looked his way and waved. Harold smiled.

'Noooooo!' Harold screamed. Elizabeth hit Barb in the back of the head, and Barb fell and kept falling into a hole in the ground. Elizabeth started to shovel soil into the ground over Barb. The children carried on running around and singing as if nothing had happened. Elizabeth now waved, with blood dripping from the knife she held. 'I did it, Harold. Shall I get the children next?'

'No, don't do it. No!' Harold was crying and trying to climb over his fence but he couldn't get over – the fence was getting higher and higher. He couldn't reach the top.

'I'll catch them – don't worry, Harold!' Elizabeth yelled. 'I'll get them.' She called them over, holding the knife behind her back. 'Jane, sweetheart, Todd, my lovely – I have a surprise for you both. Come here.'

'Jane, Todd – run! Get away from her. She wants to kill you,' Harold shouted and shouted. He closed his eyes and tried to think of something else. Was this his dream, his imagination or was he hallucinating? He knew he'd overdone it on the drugs. A cold hand struck him hard in the face. He opened his eyes and was sat back in the kitchen facing the clock. The clock ticked and ticked …

# CHAPTER FIFTY
# BARBARA
# JANUARY 1970

'He's at it again,' Barb said.

'At what? Being moody? Being a miserable man? What is he doing now? Barb's neighbour Margaret asked, and chuckled.

'You know, every year he starts thinking he's an author and he writes about some nonsense,' Barb said. 'It's always the same nonsense though.'

'Well, it causes no harm, does it?' Margaret asked, as she turned on her heels to walk home. 'I must be off; Jane shouldn't be left at home by herself for too long – she's only a baby really.'

Barb frowned. 'Quicky, go home you idiot,' she said, and waved her arm to hurry her friend up. She shut the door hard on purpose, angry her friend had left her child. She wasn't a baby, but she shouldn't have been left with no adult supervision.

March 1974

'Why are you looking after her again,' Harold grumbled, and put his head back in his book.

Barbara ignored him and gave Jane a friendly smile.

'Shall we go out for a walk to the park?' Barb asked Jane.

'Okay,' Jane said quietly.

They walked for ten minutes, with Barb doing most of the talking. Jane was a quiet girl and Barb had to really prise any information out of her, but she was determined to do just that.

'So, do you and your mum see much of Harold these days?' Barb asked.

'No, not really,' Jane said, and looked away from Barb.

'It must be weird seeing him again,' Barb said.

'My mum says Harold does what he pleases and not what pleases other people. Is that right?' Jane asked. 'My mum thinks he's a selfish man.'

Barb was a little taken aback, but although she still hated Margaret, she knew what Jane had just said was true – it had hit a nerve but it was most definitely true. After she'd found out last year that Jane was Harold's daughter, she couldn't forgive her friend and struggled to put up with Harold. Between Barb, Margaret and Harold, they'd all agreed no one must know about this. Harold wasn't even bothered about seeing Jane, but Barb had no children – they'd tried but it wasn't meant to be, she'd thought. That was the hardest part to take: she couldn't have children; she now knew that she was the problem. But this had given her an opportunity to care for another human being; it was far from ideal but she was starting to love Jane like her own. Barb made sure she was given ample time with Jane or she would make sure everyone knew about her dirty husband and his little whore. It would ruin his reputation forever – the whole community knew him as a war veteran, a hero. All this would disappear.

'What else does your mum say about Harold?' Barb said,

and then winked at Jane, which made Jane giggle.

'Not much,' Jane said. 'Have you heard Harold talking to the Utal?' she asked.

'The what?' Barb asked.

'It's a creature that tells him what to write and do; that's what he told me,' Jane said.

'I think it's Harold's way of playing with you, dear,' Barb said. 'He can be a little bit of a strange man, but this is a way of trying to play with you,' Barb said, but she wasn't sure who she was trying to reassure – Jane or herself.

'No, I don't think so,' Jane said. 'I was watching him from outside the living room and he was talking for ages. Then I came in and asked him who he was talking to and he said the Utal. I asked him where it was and he said, in front of me. I like playing make-believe – it was funny for a while, but then he was a little bit scary. He told me it wasn't make-believe and I was a stupid little girl and I didn't know anything. I couldn't see anything, honestly. Is he okay?'

Even for Harold this was weird, Barb thought.

'I'll speak to him and tell him to play nicely,' Barb said. 'I'm sorry if he scared you, love.'

'Okay then,' Jane said, and she ran ahead of Barb, with her eyes on the swings and slide in the park.

Barb was thankful Jane was only an 8-year-old; she'd forget about this and hopefully not tell her mum. But her mum must have known already how odd Harold could be. Barb needed to get Harold to the doctors; he was losing the plot – she was sure of it.

# CHAPTER FIFTY-ONE
# JUDE
# PRESENT DAY

He'd arrived at his mum's house to find his dad was also there – not ideal preparation for a new job, one with a fairly early start. It was one of those awkward situations that could be funny, if he had someone to share the moment with other than his parents. He'd thought, if he had a girlfriend then they would have a good old giggle once they got back home tonight. The reason Jude found the whole situation funny was they had something to tell him – they hadn't asked how he was or where he had been lately, or if he had a new job. No, they were just bothered about themselves and their news. Like he didn't already know what the surprise was, and how old were they to be on, off, on, off, like a couple of love-struck teenagers?

The table was set. Jude always knew something was going down when the special tablecloth was brought out; normally it was only used at Christmas or for a birthday party or, big hint, he thought, a we're back together announcement again.

There was a bottle of fizz placed as the centrepiece of the

table; this was set with the special vase that was full of fresh yellow tulips. Fizz was a new idea and this threw Jude a little bit. He thought this felt like service that he'd receive in a posh hotel, not like the God-awful hotel in Bournemouth. He had been given a glass of champagne at the front door (by his dad) that he was currently nursing; he didn't want a refill. It didn't feel like his childhood home today.

'Who is going to tell me the meaning of this charade?' Jude asked his parents. 'Come on – I can't handle the suspense anymore,' he said in a sarky tone. He looked at both of his parents and waited for their answer.

'This is not a charade, dear,' his mum said. 'We have some exciting news. Me and your dad, as you know, haven't always seen eye to eye.'

'I hadn't noticed,' Jude said. 'Come on, spit it out!'

'Don't be rude to your mother, boy,' his dad said and gave him a look.

'Anyhow, we just wanted to let you know first …' his mum began.

'You are back together again. Congratulations – have a lovely month,' Jude said. 'Some of us have other things to think about, other than your, oh, we are back together. Oh no, we split up again. Boohoo!'

He felt utterly fed up with them; he was sick of their on and off relationship. And especially how they always sucked him into it. He'd had to put up with it for years, but not anymore – he didn't need this. They were the reason he'd never had a long-term relationship; even Elizabeth had had the nerve to mock him. He had picked up their traits or he just didn't want to end up like them – he wasn't sure which one it was. Either way he'd felt embarrassed that his old wicked teacher could insult him so easily. But he didn't live with either of his parents now. So why were they still dragging him back into it?

'Like I was about to say, dear,' his mum said. She looked too happy; this was a peak point for one of her highs followed by an almighty fall, Jude thought. 'I don't say it much, we don't say it much, but we are immensely proud of you. You have created yourself a great career, a little off-track at the moment, but you'll bounce back, dear, we just know it.'

'Thanks,' Jude said. It was strange praise but he wasn't used to any from his mum. He'd turned slightly red in the face. But he wasn't fooled by their performance and his dad was oddly quiet. 'What is going on, Dad?'

'Let your mum tell you, boy,' his dad said.

'It's exciting news,' his mum said. Just then, it dawned on him. She was too old – surely not. They couldn't be. Could they?

'I know, and we know, we haven't always been the best parents,' his mum said. 'But we have always shown you love and you have never gone without – we have always tried our best.'

'Don't say it,' Jude said. 'Please don't – you can't. It wouldn't be fair on them.'

'Don't be rude, boy,' his dad said again. Jude wondered if his dad had got stuck on repeat tonight.

'You're going to be an amazing big brother, dear,' his mum said. She looked at his dad and then gave him a big hug and kiss.

'Well, boy, what do you say?' his dad said. Jude was lost for words and felt a little sick. He couldn't think of anything positive to say.

There were many things going through his head. He wanted to say, 'what happens when you break up?' As it was inevitable. Will I end up looking after him? That is the most likely outcome, he thought. His mum had told him many times how he was the only reason she kept going – would she mentally torture this unborn child in the future? Do they have it in them to go through parenting all over again? Should I report them? Report them to who? But he said none of those and didn't ask one question.

'Do you know the phrase you both taught me when growing up?' Jude asked rhetorically. 'If you don't have anything positive to say, then don't say anything at all. That sums up this ridiculous situation the best, I believe.'

And with that, he said goodnight and left for home.

# CHAPTER FIFTY-TWO
## LEWIS

'What is all that racket, Lewis?' Lewis' mum Jane complained, as she shouted up the stairs at him. 'Would you stop making all that awful noise right now. I'm not asking you again. Stop it right now or else.'

Lewis was lying down on his bed. He threw a tennis ball, bouncing it against the ceiling, one last time and let it fall on to his bedroom floor. It settled amongst a pile of his dirty clothes. He looked at his phone and fired off a short text to Jay: 'Bruv, are we still on?' The dots came up on his phone; he could see his friend was replying immediately.

'Why not? Let's go,' Jay texted him back within seconds.

Lewis looked around his room, grabbed his house keys off his bedside table and then rustled around with his school blazer until he found a milk chocolate Bounty bar, which he'd stolen from the 'All in One Shop' next to his school. He stuffed one of the two pieces in his mouth whilst he looked at his phone again. 'Be there in five mins, mate,' Lewis texted Jay back. He picked up the photo book he kept under his bed and looked through his photos, stopping on an old one that his mum had given to him. It was of Harold and his wife Barbara stood beside him; they held a little baby wrapped in a pink blanket.

'You mug – disrespect me,' Lewis mumbled. And he quickly closed the book and put it back under his bed.

'Mum!' Lewis shouted, whilst standing and looking over the banister of the stairs. 'Mum!' Lewis shouted again impatiently.

'Yeah – what now?' his mum asked.

'I'm going out. Don't cook me any dinner tonight,' Lewis said.

'Too late for that,' his mum said. 'It's already cooking in the oven and you'll eat if you're hungry or not.'

Lewis was finishing the other half of his Bounty bar as he stomped down the stairs. He put his bashed-up white trainers on and picked up his football. 'Leave it on the kitchen side and I'll eat it when I get in then.'

'I can see you're hungry enough eating something and you shouldn't talk with your mouthful. How many times do I have to repeat myself?' his mum said. 'It's rude and I've brought you up better than that.'

'Okay, Mum. Don't moan at me and don't wait up either,' Lewis said, and gave his mum a cheeky wink.

'You'll be in when I bloody well tell you to be home – no later than 9,' she said.

Lewis waved as he opened the front door and walked off. 'What's that, Mum. I can't hear you. Yes, see you tomorrow,' Lewis said.

'If you weren't so damn cute, I'd throttle you,' his mum said, as she walked over to close the door behind him.

Lewis smiled. 'Love you too, Mum.' He waved once more, walked off and didn't look back.

# CHAPTER FIFTY-THREE
# LEWIS

He ran along the pavement kicking his football until he had done one too many kick-ups and lost control of the ball. He then chased after it and bumped into a woman, not looking where he was going – his eyes were only on the ball. He got a shock when the woman's Rottweiler barked and jumped up at him.

'Sorry, I didn't mean to,' Lewis said, and backed away from the moody-looking woman and her huge dog.

'Come on, Steve,' the woman said to her dog, and carried on walking, not even acknowledging Lewis.

Lewis laughed. 'Steve, a dog called Steve,' Lewis said, and shook his head laughing as he continued to walk towards Harold's house. The serious woman had reminded him of her, the lady who said her name was Sarah. But Lewis was sure that wasn't her real name. His phone buzzed.

'I'm there already. Come on, bro, hurry up,' the text read – it was from Jay. He was at the park behind Harold's house. Lewis didn't reply and put his phone back in his pocket – he in fact walked a little bit slower. He thought about what Sarah had told him, and the more he thought about her the stranger she was. The fact she had handwritten to him to meet was odd enough – who writes anything these days? he'd thought. The letter he'd received was in a waxed sealed envelope, which he'd found even more peculiar.

He'd met up with her, as she'd instructed, outside an old pub that had seen better days – a lot of the letters had fallen off the sign that stood above the front door. It surely wasn't meant to be called the Sun Hip, but she'd said meet at the pub on Hive Avenue, and this was the only pub. When she arrived, she wore a black beret and a pair of tortoiseshell sunglasses with dark lenses. He couldn't see her eyes; he didn't trust her.

She didn't say hello, but just started to talk. 'Harold or your grandad or whatever you like to call him,' she said. 'I can't be sure, but I'd place money on him asking you to be his follower.'

At the time he'd just nodded; he thought she was mad and he just wanted to get away from her and go back home. Her odd appearance made her look like if he didn't agree, she'd pull a weapon out her jacket and stab him to death. So, he went along with what she had to say, even though he thought it was a load of rubbish.

A few days later, Lewis couldn't believe it – Harold did what she said. But he had no intention of going through with her plans. He had his own ideas; he had a better plan.

# CHAPTER FIFTY-FOUR
# HAROLD
# ON THE DAY
# PART TWO

Harold had fallen asleep. He had been mumbling to himself in his sleep, and was abruptly awoken by an almighty crash; he then heard Lewis and Jay both shouting outside. Harold stretched – he'd hurt his neck again sleeping awkwardly on the table. He looked towards the clock but then remembered time stood still; but as he woke up and rubbed his eyes, he could see time was ticking faster than ever. He thought the meds must have knocked him out; no way would he normally fall asleep at the table. It was dark outside and the rain was thumping down. He opened the back door and peered into his garden. He rubbed his eyes; they were red and had dark patches under them. He could see the ball in his garden. He tried to steady his shakes, and shook his head waking himself up. He gripped the handle of the baseball bat; his hands were sweaty but he held it as tightly as he could. He could hear Lewis and Jay arguing about who would jump over the fence to get the ball. He hoped Lewis could convince Jay as he wasn't sure he would recognise who was who in the dark.

The rain bounced down harder, hitting Harold continually as he crept towards the fence. Darkness rose above him and two figures jumped simultaneously over it. It was unexpected – Harold staggered backwards.

'What are you going to do with a bat, old man,' Jay shouted at Harold, as he fast approached him. 'I know about your plan to scare me. Who's laughing now, old man?'

'Yes, old man. What you going to do?' Lewis said, and smirked at Harold. 'Old man is crazy, you know, bruv.'

'I thought you …' Harold began.

'What? You thought that I was crazy too? That I would believe in your mental book. No, old man, I don't, you old fool. Get him, Jay,' Lewis ordered.

Harold held the bat tight and swung at the air as Jay started to get nearer to him. The bat hit Jay on his shoulder, but the impact didn't stop him as he continued forwards. He pulled the bat out of Harold's hands easily.

'He's only gone and pissed himself, stupid old …' Jay started to say.

'Throw me the bat,' Lewis said.

'Alight, alight,' Jay said, not taking his eyes off Harold as he learnt backwards and handed the bat to Lewis.

Harold could now see who the leader was. He now knew for sure when Lewis' mum had told him about a bully at school, she wasn't talking about Jay or anyone else. She was talking about Lewis. Jay pulled Harold to his feet.

Harold's vision blurred as the impact hit him. He fell hard, hitting the back of his head. The weight pressed down on him; he tried to move, but he was too heavy, a dead weight. He shivered. He was cold, but hot redness was spreading on his chest. He couldn't work out if it was his blood or not. Had Jay stabbed him?

He looked up at Lewis, who towered over him holding the baseball bat. He now understood what had happened as Jay's lifeless body lay on top of him.

He thought Lewis was about to help him up, but he then couldn't see him anymore and time really did seem to stop or go in slow motion as he struggled for breath under the weight of Jay. He could hear someone gagging or being sick close by; he guessed it was Lewis, but couldn't be sure.

# CHAPTER FIFTY-FIVE
# THE WRITER

The butterfly flutters and glides, exuberant colours and pollen fill its senses and dark red petals reflect against its symmetrical wings. Through its spiracles, oxygen pulsates through its body; life is beautiful, with not a care in the world.

Life hadn't always been this way. The end was the beginning, as the words he'd longed to hear resonated through his mind. He was cleansed and all of his faults and sins faded and kept doing so until they were completely diluted and disappeared. And his life began.

The wax stamp hit the envelope; it was ready to post. One last letter.

# CHAPTER FIFTY-SIX
# JUDE
# THE RADIO

There were only a few minutes of preparation left – this was it, the start of his new career. It was 5.58am and *People Issues* went live for its first show in just two minutes' time. Jude was relieved as he now knew he didn't have to put his new role in any jeopardy and didn't have to risk his friendship with Nigel. He had spoken with Tiff last night – she'd called him with some good and bad news of her own.

What didn't bode too well for the first show was how exhausted Jude felt; he was struggling to keep his eyes from closing.

Last night, first he had to deal with the God-awful news from his parents and then once he'd driven back home, he sat in his lounge and had a dram of Scotch and tried his best to relax. He waited for his initial anger to subside before making his way up to bed. He brushed his teeth, poured a glass of cold water and put it on his bedside table, then stripped off, only wearing a T-shirt and his boxers as he climbed into bed. He was warm under his covers. He looked at his phone, set his alarm clock for the early start and tried not to think about how little sleep he was about to get. He was finally relaxing when he went to put his phone down and it started to buzz. He talked to Tiff into the early hours; he'd barely managed a couple of hours of sleep when his alarm clock annoyingly woke him up.

'Welcome to our first show and we hope the start of something special. My name is Jude Holmes and this is *People Issues* coming to you live at 6am,' Jude announced. He had been nervous coming in in the morning but felt confident in his new role, as the theme music of his new show played. Nigel was in the studio and had made Jude feel comfortable before going live, and he was only a stone's throw away if needed.

'We have a schedule that my boss and old pal Nigel would like to stick to. But I will interrupt this schedule for one minute with some breaking news, coming to you first from *People Issues*,' Jude said. He could see Nigel looking at him in surprise.

'Last night, local police had a breakthrough in the murder case of Barbara Larkin, the late wife of well-respected resident, Harold Larkin,' Jude said. 'And an old teacher of mine, Elizabeth Beecham, who many people of a similar age to me may remember, last night gave evidence to the police. She has admitted she and Harold killed Barbara. She has since given the police the location of where the victim's body was buried. The garden of the house she used to live in has been excavated and a body was found. *People Issues* has been informed Elizabeth Beecham and Harold Larkin have both been arrested for the murder of Barbara Larkin.'

Jude looked up at Nigel and the rest of the team; they hadn't cut him off air so that was a good sign. All of them looked busy on their phones, probably looking for another news outlet that would confirm what Jude was telling them right now. He could see Nigel looked unhappy and was shaking his head, but Jude knew this time he was right, and everything was going to be okay. This would in fact be the making of the show – he was sure of it.

He cleared his throat and continued. 'I can also bring you it here first on *People Issues*. They, Harold and Elizabeth, have also been arrested for the attempted murder of Elizabeth's son at the time,' Jude said. 'In light of all this new evidence and some unspecified further developments with the Jay Whittle inquiry, Harold is a person of great interest for his involvement in the attempted murder of Jay.' He stopped for breath, before opening the lines for callers.

After the adrenaline of the show wore off, Jude was exhausted and spent the majority of the rest of the day catching up on some much-needed sleep. After he'd woken up and eaten a ham and mustard sandwich and drank a few cups of hot coffee, he sat in his study spinning on his chair. He stopped, leant across his pine desk and dipped the nib of his fountain pen into a deep blue bottle of ink; he twisted the piston and then wiped away the residue ink. He eyed the crisp, empty white sheet of paper that sat in front of him.

'Okay, this will be the truth,' he said, and began to write.

His phone began to ring – the name Tiff was on his screen. They spoke for around ten minutes; Tiff cried and she cried some more. The police had informed her the body of Barbara had been found; her mum was right – they had buried her in what was Tiff's childhood house. The police had also informed Tiff that Elizabeth was not a suspect and had no involvement in what was now a murder enquiry, for the murder of Jay Whittle.

Jude felt dreadful; he felt pained and upset but he knew he couldn't even comprehend the type of agony Jay's parents were feeling right now. But he did know more than ever it was important to write what he saw that night. He put his pen to paper again.

# CHAPTER FIFTY-SEVEN
## BARBARA

'Is it me, or what is it?' Barb asked. 'I'm old – I'm too old now, is that it?'

'No, it's not like that. I'm not having an affair – don't be silly,' Harold said.

'Am I stupid?' Barb asked. 'Is that what you think? You do, don't you. You always have. At first, we were the perfect couple. I'd hear people, random old women, say, "aren't they cute". Then after a few years of marriage and no children, people didn't look at us all adoringly anymore. They still looked at us; they all looked at us. I could feel their eyes burning on my skin.'

'Barb, come on – it's not like that. No one ...' Harold tried to interrupt her.

'Don't. Just don't,' Barb said. 'I tried not to look into their eyes at first, but these people, these regular shopkeepers, neighbours, aunties and mums. God damn mums who were somehow bloody pregnant again – they weren't going away. One day, I'd had enough – the whole situation had got to me. It was our neighbour Sally. She only said the usual.'

'When will we see a little sprog, a miniature you running

around or a little Harold,' Sally asked. 'Ohh, that would be adorable. Wouldn't that be bliss? That's the dream, isn't it?'

'And I said the usual,' Barb said. 'I said, "I'm not sure. We've a lot going on in our lives, what with Harold's work – he has a very important job as you know and it takes up a lot of his time. I'm not sure we'd have the time," I said to her. We would – I know that; we know that. She kept nodding her stupid little head and her eyes, they were the worst part. She knew – I looked straight into her murky green eyes and they pierced my heart like a knife. I came home and cried all day and then into the night. The worst part was you. You came to bed late that night and didn't say one word. Not a word – not one word. Do you know how hurtful that is?'

'I didn't know,' Harold said. 'How am I supposed to know you talked to a witch that can tell your thoughts, for goodness' sake. This is ridiculous.'

'Are you making fun of me now? Really – are you that insensitive?' Barb asked. 'Because the way I see it is you go around sleeping with loads of other women and I deal with the consequences – I pick up all your mess. You can't take it. We can't have children – I can't have children – so you sow your seed with anyone and everyone you can. That's what I see. Who is she, this Lizzy?'

'Elizabeth is a friend,' Harold said, and took a seat, shaking his head, quietly mumbling and swearing to himself.

'You're going to go quiet now, like I'm the one with the problems,' Barb said, and swiped some newspapers off the kitchen side on to the floor.

'If you're going to talk rubbish, can you blame me?' Harold said.

'I put my heart on the table,' Barb said. 'I say how I feel, how betrayed I feel right now, and you call it rubbish? How dare you.'

'Rubbish.' Harold shrugged his shoulders and looked

away from Barb nonchalantly.

'I'll give you rubbish,' Barb said. 'The drivel you have been writing – you know, some of our neighbours avoid you. I've heard them talking – everyone in this street thinks you've lost the plot. I actually defended you; I am always defending you. That's how stupid I am.'

'If the shoe fits,' Harold said. 'You don't know what you're talking about. The Book of Truth – you think this is rubbish?' Harold jumped up from his seat, threw the seat and it crashed hard against the wall.

'Such an ironic name – you wouldn't know the truth if it hit you in the face,' Barb said, and opened the back door, walked out and slammed it behind her.

'Rat ... vermin ... diseased ... plagued,' the Utal whispered in Harold's ear.

# CHAPTER FIFTY-EIGHT
# LEWIS

The police dropped Lewis at his home. They informed his mum about Jay and how he was taken away in an ambulance, how his parents had been called and how Harold had been arrested. Lewis felt like a sandwich all wrapped up in a foil jacket – it was put on him by one of the officers to keep him warm. They told him he was in shock and asked his mum to make him a tea with sugar and biscuits.

'We need to talk – sit down,' his mum Jane said. 'Don't walk away from me.'

'Talk about what?' Lewis said. 'I'm going up to bed. I'm tired – I need to go to bed.'

'About tonight – what do you think?' his mum said. 'Your friend is in hospital and in a serious condition. We need to talk about Harold being arrested. About your grandad, about what happened. The list goes on. And your tea is here.'

'Easy – Jay's not my friend,' Lewis said. 'And Harold technically might be my grandad but he's not really, is he? He doesn't want to be and I don't want him to be. And last of all, tonight was nothing. Are we done? Can I go to bed?' Lewis said, and walked over and picked up his tea and a few chocolate Bourbons to take to bed with him.

'I'm speechless,' his mum said. Lewis had now climbed a few steps to go upstairs. 'When did you get such a cold heart? The son I brought up had feelings. I don't know this Lewis – this is not my Lewis.'

'Goodnight,' Lewis said, shaking his head and looking away from his mum. He walked upstairs and straight into his bedroom, closing the door behind him and locking it. He sat on his bed, wishing he did have more emotion. He thought about Jay; he liked him but he was stupid and would always go along with all his crazy ideas. He was a sheep and he'd follow the other sheep to slaughter.

At first, when they met at school, Jay had taunted him in front of their classmates for being poor. Lewis was quiet, unassuming, a target for a bully like Jay. Lewis waited until the end of the day and beat Jay in front of the same classmates, punching him repeatedly until another brave classmate asked him to stop. He then made him give him his shoes and socks.

'Who's poor now?' Lewis said. 'Go home and tell your parents you've given me your shoes and socks because I'm poor and I need them more than you. Be convincing or, well, you know what will happen if they don't believe you – I'll beat you tomorrow and the day after that.' The next day, Jay had new shoes and no one in the class, and no teacher or parent, said anything to Lewis. Lewis didn't have many friends (after what he'd done to Jay, most of his class were too scared to talk to him) and he liked the way Jay would suck up to him – he would do anything he said. In Harold's garden, he'd hit Jay harder than he'd meant to, but he was young and strong – he'd be fine, Lewis thought. There was a bigger picture that Jay knew nothing about, but if he knew what Harold was capable of, then he would have understood.

Lewis felt around under his bed until his hand touched the dusty old book. Once the book was sat on his lap, he brushed the cover with his sleeve until he could see the words the Book of Truth. He'd seen it lying next to the shed when that pesky Jade or Jude or whoever he was turned up, and when he'd finally managed to persuade Jude to leave, he picked it up. He stood with Harold waiting for the ambulance to arrive. He told Harold the book now belonged to him and if he tried stop him, then he'd end up in an ambulance as well.

'I can't let you have it,' Harold said. 'This is my property and no one else's – besides, it's a bad idea. Now go and put it back in the house where it belongs.'

'No, this book belongs to me now,' Lewis told him. 'You are a stupid old man. You either have a selective memory or you're plain dumb. You don't even know who I am, do you.'

'My memory isn't the best, I'll admit, you're right, but I know who you are alright. Now give me the book back – it is mine,' Harold said, and tugged Lewis' arm.

'Do you?' Lewis asked. 'Really? Then who is my mum? Who is she to you, old man?'

'Don't be silly – I don't have the time for this,' Harold said, and stopped talking for a moment whilst Lewis glared at him

'Who is she?' Lewis said louder. 'Tell me who she is – now.'

'She, she is … a lovely lady who helps me …' Harold stuttered.

Lewis moved the book away as Harold tried to snatch it from his hands. He pushed Harold back to the ground, the ground he'd not long picked him up from. He felt enraged and kicked dirt into Harold's face. He stopped himself from repeatedly kicking him.

'You're ancient and feeble – I should feel sorry for you,' Lewis said. 'But I know who you really are – you are the scum of the earth, that's what you are, and you don't even deserve my hate.'

Lewis looked at him and watched as Harold wiped dirt from his forehead and out of his eyes. He leant against the fence trying to calm himself and not look at Harold too much. He didn't want to help him back up again. He knew he was desperately old and feeble. They were waiting for an ambulance and probably the police from the sound of the operator's voice, but he didn't care if Harold just died right there and then.

'You know it's for the best, that I wasn't too involved with her upbringing,' Harold said. 'I'm a bad person – you're right.'

Lewis was stunned; he wasn't sure what to say.

'Okay, I'm going to tell you something,' Harold said. 'It's your choice. I'm not the man I used to be – the way you've pushed me around tonight is all the proof you need – so I can't stop you. But if you take that book, I promise you you'll regret it – it would be the worst decision of your life.'

The sound of the sirens was getting closer. Lewis held the book out to give it back to Harold. There was more noise, screeches of wheels and the slamming of car doors coming from the front of the house. Lewis panicked and threw the book up and over the fence.

'Leave the book there,' Harold said. 'I'll go and get it tomorrow, don't worry.'

Shortly after Harold was arrested, Lewis told the police lady who was comforting him that he thought he'd dropped his school work earlier when he was playing football with his friend Jay. She was more than happy to oblige and to go and have a look for his work. After walking around for a few minutes, they both agreed it looked like his book was the only thing they could find. Maybe the rest had blown away. It was too dark to be looking and, more importantly, the police lady needed to get him home to his mum. 'His school surely will understand the situation,' she said. He agreed and said he was tired, and wanted go home, warm up and see his mum.

Waiting until his mum was asleep, he crept downstairs and unlocked the back door; he had a bottle of lighter fluid, some matches and the book. Lewis stood in his garden with his big navy puffer jacket on and a pair of woolly gloves, but he was still cold and shaking. He noticed as he held it out in front of his eyes that the book he'd only recently cleaned was still dusty. He knew how much this book meant to Harold. He'd read the scriptures; the police would know how crazy Harold was even without having the Book of Truth as well – they'd surely find the scriptures in Harold's house. They'd be searching his house from top to bottom – who knows what else they'd find? Through sheer hate for his grandad, the one he now knew for sure knew who he was, he wanted to burn the Book of Truth. His grandad would still rot in jail, he hoped. The flames of the fire flickered in the wind and he dropped the book on top. 'Good riddance,' he said as he watched the book glisten and glow in the dark until it burnt into smithereens.

# CHAPTER FIFTY-NINE
# JUDE

The scream – the sound sent shudders down his spine; it would live in his nightmares forever. Regrettably but instinctively, he sprinted towards the noise. When he heard the scream, his first thoughts were this was a woman being attacked. Jude was out jogging – it was raining hard and he was soaked. He'd been out running for half an hour already and had been thinking of giving a last effort and trying to sprint home, if his body would allow him to. But his plans changed.

By the time he'd got to the scene of what he now knew was one of a premeditated murder, he was completely out of breath. It was dark but not pitch black; he could see well enough to know what he was seeing. What he saw next made his stomach turn; he heaved whilst still trying to catch his breath, which was a difficult feat, and it came out as an odd, pig-like oink sound.

At first they didn't see him, but it didn't take long and when they did, they dropped him and his body hit the soil, lifeless with a dull thud, and some blood splattered on to the fences. That was when the pleading began, the insistent begging. He walked backwards; he couldn't quite believe what he'd seen – Harold with his hunched-over frame had been struggling, but he'd been holding Jay under Jay's arms and Lewis had held his legs. Jay's backside was being dragged along on the ground – the gate was about to close behind Lewis, but Jude had caught Harold's eye, and Harold dropped Jay and Lewis staggered backwards, somehow managing to stay on his feet.

Jude quickly pulled out his phone and started to dial for an ambulance or the police or both – he wasn't sure. Lewis shouted, 'Stop!', and said he'd call them instead.

'I was just about to call them anyway,' Lewis said, and proceeded to dial for an ambulance from his phone.

Jude listened in as Lewis spoke on the phone to the operator and explained where they were.

'It was just an accident,' Harold said. 'These things can happen.'

'I'm sure. Have you checked his pulse?' Jude asked. 'Is he breathing?' Jude watched as he and Harold shared an odd exchange in glances. Harold then was the one who checked Jay's pulse.

'He has a pulse,' Harold said. 'It does seem slow though, but what do I know?' He went back into the house, grabbed a blanket and rushed back over and wrapped Jay up.

'You see, I have a bad reputation at school and the police will think I did this on purpose,' Lewis said.

'I'm sure they won't – the police aren't biased and won't be asking for your school reports,' Jude said.

'They all stick together – you don't know,' Lewis said.

Harold interrupted. 'I'm old – if anyone is to get into trouble, it'll be me,' he said. 'I'll take the blame – it's better that way. Anyway, it was an accident and Jay will tell them when he's better. Won't he, Lewis?'

'Sure,' Lewis said.

Harold, for some reason, knew who Jude was and told him to write the story. He explained to Jude how he couldn't tell who was in his garden and was scared. He'd lashed out; he didn't mean to hurt anyone. The conversation continued, until Jude heard sirens faintly in the distance and Harold convinced him it was better that Jude left the scene. He did leave but before he went home, he stood around the corner for what seemed like a lifetime. He could hear Lewis and Harold arguing but couldn't make out what they were bickering about. He waited until he saw paramedics with Jay. He'd seen Jay's chest rising and deflating – he was at least breathing. Jude was relieved; Harold had told him the truth about that at least.

Jude made it home. He showered, ate beans on toast with brown sauce and tried to warm up. Once he'd changed and warmed up, he sat down on his sofa with a hot cup of tea. Afterwards, he went over to his study and settled at his desk with his laptop. He made sure his report made it clear that Harold was the attacker. Harold had been right – Lewis was young – and they both said it was an accident.

Thinking back, his report was always doomed. He now knew why Harold and Lewis didn't want him to call the ambulance and why they both wanted him to go – this meant there would be no witnesses seen at the crime. Harold was respected in the community – his report wouldn't stick – but what he hadn't counted on was the forensics, the prints, Lewis' prints all over the bat. Or maybe he knew Lewis would be arrested and that is why he paid for his solicitor fees and continued with his side of the story in the press: he was old and wasn't exactly sure what happened on the night; maybe he did it – he was frail and frightened and was just protecting his home; he didn't mean to hurt anyone though. Or he did do it – he just couldn't remember. It all happened so quickly, he'd said, changing his story every time, playing on the fact his mind wasn't quite with it. Jude was sure Harold was hoping for everyone to be sympathetic because of his age and ignore everything else.

Jay Whittle died from the attack and Harold had since been arrested for a historic murder. What Jude had previously written about wasn't a story that was biased and out to get a local hero, like his boss originally said before dismissing him. It was much more than that, and Jude now knew what really happened that night – Lewis and Harold had planned this murder. But they both had very different motives.

Jude started to write:

When you reach your 70s, 80s or in Harold's case 90s, you'll not have the same memory as you once did in your youth. Lewis' mum used to visit Harold and help him around the house. She'd cook his meals and do some cleaning, like any good neighbour or long-standing friend would, or a family member would, like a daughter. This was the part, the key part, that was missing. Harold knew and so did Lewis' mum, although they never spoke about it anymore. It was a sore subject. Lewis' mum Jane was indeed Harold's daughter. Barbara knew about her, and Harold at the time knew about Barbara and Jane's relationship. He knew Barbara would see Jane and take her out but didn't know the depth of their bond. They spoke about everything. You see, when Barbara's body was discovered, this didn't just bring to life an old case, it brought to life a new case. Harold's house also had to be searched and what they found amongst other possibly more disturbing material was an old diary, Barbara's old diary. It contained the daily conversations that Jane and Barbara used to have. Like the time Barbara told Jane that her and her husband Harold had been to hospital for him to undergo tests for his memory again and they still couldn't find anything wrong. The diary later explained that Harold had said all the tests came back fine and he had nothing wrong with his brain; his memory was just fine, he'd said. It also mentioned how, since the tests, Harold had become more and more distant, how he'd started to write again, carry around the book and talk to himself.

# CHAPTER SIXTY
## JUDE

Jude had kept in contact with Tiff on a daily basis since they had first met. Tiff had told Jude about Jane and that she knew she was Harold's daughter. He'd asked her if her mum was also Jane's mum, but she wasn't, according to Tiff. But Tiff knew of Jane's existence and how her mum had been jealous of all of Harold's interests in other women around that time. Tiff mentioned a woman called Margaret, and gave Jude the number of an unnamed policeman she'd been talking to. And, after surprisingly little persuasion, he got an interview with this officer.

They talked for a few hours, but the policeman, for obvious reasons, didn't want his name to be taken. He said to Jude that if he could find the information that he was about to give him through different sources, then he could use this information, but to not use this conversation as the source. He made some smirky remark about Jude not being a journalist anymore and how no one got up early enough to listen to him in the morning anyhow, and that was why he didn't mind talking to him. Jude knew this wasn't the reason; he was corrupt, and Tiff must have had something on him, he was sure.

He told Jude there was enough medicine found in Harold's house to start a pharmacy. He laughed and Jude laughed, but Jude knew this was no laughing matter – they were talking about a killer. A possible serial killer.

'Amongst the treasure case of medicines,' the police officer said, laughing at his own joke, 'what we found was a medicine called L-Dopa – this is used for patients with varying forms of dementia. If self-diagnosed, this medicine can cause you to have hallucinations.' Jude checked this out – in fact he googled it – and the policeman was right.

He said all the talk down the station was that they all knew it was Harold. The only reason he had been released previously was some cock-up with forensics with the prints on the bat. This had put Lewis in the frame, but they all knew it was Harold – there was no doubt. And when they searched his house and found loads of crazy books called the scriptures and some strange letters, this cemented what all the guys at the station thought all along. The police officer told Jude there were even lots of notes dotted around the house written about killing the sacrifice and how Lewis would bring him this sacrifice.

'He'd even written down that Jay would be the sacrifice. You don't get much more concrete evidence than that,' the police officer said.

The thing was, Jude knew the actual truth and the police were wrong – Lewis was the killer. Harold knew this too, but he would never say it was Lewis who killed Jay.

The reason for Jude's dishonesty with the police, or his just not telling them the truth, was he knew what he saw on the night when he got to the scene of the crime. He could see in Harold's eyes a man who had been caught, a murderer. And what he also saw, and hoped he saw in Lewis' eyes, was a young man who had made a mistake. Lewis called the

ambulance and had tears running down his face, and looked
to Jude a young man who was trying to right a wrong, a child
who had tried to impress his grandad.

Jude had spoken with Jane, and she said Lewis had told
her that Harold and Lewis had chatted for hours one night
about the lost years and how Harold would make amends.
But Lewis was so upset a few nights later when Harold
couldn't remember a thing and rejected the fact that he was
his grandson when Lewis mentioned it again.

Harold was a murderer; he may not have killed Jay, but
that didn't mean he hadn't planned to. In Lewis there was
still some hope.

Jude finished writing everything up he now knew and
signed off – Jude Holmes. But this time he wasn't going to
make the same mistake as before. He was sure as hell he
wasn't going to take his report to the local gazette and let Mr
Tomkins take any glory – no, there was no glory to be had.
Innocent people had died and now at last justice would be
served and that was the best outcome; no article would ever
come close.

Sitting in his garden, he breathed in the cold night air; he
poked at the fire with an old rusted pair of prongs. He
chucked some old wood on to his brickwork barbecue – it
crackled and flames flickered. He thought of Jay and the
sadness his parents must have been going through. He held
Dylan close to him, hoping he could feel his love, and
brushed away a few tears.

He pressed the papers into the fire and pushed them
down with the old prongs. Amongst the embers, he could
see the word *truth* looking back up at him. He gave a wry
smile as he said out loud the word, 'Published'.

He looked at Dylan and asked him a question. 'The only
part I can't work out is who screamed? Can you, boy?'

Not surprisingly, Dylan didn't answer.

'You see, Dylan, I ran over that night because somebody screamed,' Jude said. 'And I'm no policeman, but if you get hit unexpectedly in the back of the head with a baseball bat then you don't get the chance to scream, do you, boy?'

Dylan looked at Jude with a puzzled expression that was mirrored by Jude.

# CHAPTER SIXY-ONE
# ARTHUR

After he'd left Big Sam's coffee house, he felt enraged – this was all Harold's fault, he thought. He jumped in his car and drove way above the speed limit all the way until he got to Harold's house. He parked a couple of doorsteps away from his house, but kept it in sight. He sat in his car and contemplated what he should do next. His initial anger after the police had questioned him and then left him to pay the bill in the coffee house had slightly subsided, but he could still feel his heart thumping.

The anger was always there, but he'd learnt to lock it away deep inside the depths of his heart, boiling and brewing. It would always be there unless he did something about it. This was his time to get his revenge for his dad.

He should have taken him down when he was younger, but he was too young at the time. Late one night, he'd overhead his grandad chatting with a returning neighbour, a war hero. For a while they were all happy and had a few drinks together, but then the conversation turned serious when they started talking about his dad.

'What happened out there, do you know?' his grandad asked.

'I can't say for sure as I wasn't there,' the neighbour said. 'But it's well known in his division about Harold – he's a coward.'

The conversation continued and the neighbour mentioned Harold had done a few standout things to let down his regiment, but he didn't elaborate. But he'd heard from people he trusted that in this particular battle, although he wasn't there so couldn't be certain, it was Harold again who had let the team down.

He said Arthur's dad had died because of Harold – he would have come home if it weren't for him and his cowardly actions or lack of actions. This had been with Arthur his whole life, but with his grandparents not having the same interest in his life when he was a child as Harold, he'd put the conversation he'd overheard down to gossip or maybe mishearing them. But all these years later, now with the police in the picture, he'd been questioned, and after Harold had blackmailed him and what he'd put him through, he thought more and more about if it was true. What if Harold's actions had killed his dad? What if Harold was the real reason he'd never had a dad growing up?

Arthur looked at his phone – his wife was calling him but he didn't answer. He checked and he had three missed calls from her. What would she do with him in jail for killing a man, who couldn't be too far away from death already. What would be the point? Okay, he'd decided he would block Harold's number and that would be that; he'd go home to his wife. He'd take care of her and love her like he always had done. He'd phone her back and tell her he was on his way back home. He was just about to press the call button.

The sound of engines and loud sirens filled his ears. He put his phone back in his pocket and ducked down on his seat.

Before he'd hidden, he had seen at least four police cars speeding his way. They screeched and then Arthur heard their car doors slam as they all rushed out. But no one approached his car – he waited and still no one approached him. They weren't here for him; he breathed a sigh of relief. But if they weren't here for him then they must have been here for Harold, he thought. His phone buzzed again – a text from Harold came up. He clicked on to the text and it was just an emoji winking. He was more confused than ever, and sat back up in his seat and looked around. The police were knocking down Harold's front door. A minute or two later, Harold was escorted out, his hands cuffed behind his back. He looked over to Arthur's car and Arthur was sure he could see Harold wink. He knew I was here but did he know what I was thinking of doing? He couldn't have, could he? Was he happy that the police had got to him first? Arthur waited for the police to drive off with Harold, before he went back home to see his wife.

A few months later, Harold had been convicted; he'd never see the light of day again. Arthur knew Harold was weird, a coward and a manipulator, but he didn't know he was capable of such a calculated, evil act. He believed that when he was child, what he'd heard the neighbour say that night about his dad to his grandad was true: Harold had been responsible for his dad's death. He never spoke to Harold like he'd wanted to and would have to live with never knowing the full extent of the truth. But with Harold in jail, he could at last live without the feeling of being watched and constantly being taunted and manipulated. He could enjoy the time he had left with his wife and rest his shoulders and relax, just a little.

# CHAPTER SIXTY-TWO
# HAROLD

He was laying down in his new bed after spending his first night in it. It was uncomfortable and hard; it hurt his back and he had woken up with a sore neck. The cell smelt like it had recently had a fresh coat of paint. The walls and ceiling were white; in the corner he had a dull beige toilet and sink that didn't look so fresh, but at least they were fairly clean. The room wasn't cold but Harold didn't feel warm either – the place felt damp. He had no chance of ever seeing freedom again. He'd been convicted for the murders of Barbara Larkin, his wife, and Jay Whittle, and the attempted murder of Todd, who was now called Tiff Beecham. He was surprised it had taken this long, in all honesty, for the police to catch up with him; he thought he should have been put in prison a long time ago. He knew what he deserved – karma had finally caught up with him. But he was petrified the Utal wouldn't see it this way.

He was disappointed Elizabeth had got away from justice – she had died two days before sentencing. He thought about her death and how it was a lucky escape.

First of all, Harold thought he'd avoid being locked away

in prison. He hoped after medical assessments they would put him in a mental home, or say he wasn't medically fit and he would go into a hospital or hospice. Not that any of these outcomes would be much better, but he was sure they would be an improvement on this drab, soul-sapping cell. The doctor's view was that Harold was very well for his age and could live for many more years yet. Harold argued he had memory issues and wasn't right mentally; he was seeing and hearing things. The doctors disagreed and said there was nothing wrong with his memory, and the only reason he'd had hallucinations was because of his self-medicating. He'd been ordering medicine on the internet for dementia and taking well over the recommended dosage for a condition he didn't actually have, multiple doctors agreed.

Harold had asked for a paper and pen but his request was denied. He hoped he could talk to the Utal. He hoped it would give him solace and reward for his work, tell him it had been worth it. He'd saved everyone and the world wasn't doomed anymore because he had given it the sacrifice. And after this life, he would be rewarded in afterlife or would be given eternal life, but not in this cell. He wanted something, just something, some comfort. He needed it. But mostly, he just wanted what he'd earned: his wife's forgiveness.

For the next week and for every night until he died at the age of 107, for every night for the fourteen years he spent in jail, he was visited.

'It's me,' she said.

'No, you're not here,' Harold said, and covered his eyes.

'But Harold, I'm here,' she said. 'You can feel me; I can feel you. I can hurt you just like you hurt me.'

'It was the Utal,' Harold said. 'It wasn't me. Don't do this, please. The Utal said you'd forgive me.'

'The Utal is your creation, Harold,' she said, 'so that you could act out your sick dreams. Now there is no Utal in prison and I'll visit you. There will be no forgiveness – I don't forgive you.'

Harold felt her nails digging into his skin, putting her weight on him and crawling up his body, getting closer to his face. She clawed at his chest and pulled herself up so she was face to face with him.

'Open your eyes, Harold. I am not real,' she said. 'All you need to do is open your eyes and think, she isn't here.'

He knew she was right, but when he woke every morning with new scratches and cuts over his body, he found it hard to believe. He opened his eyes and looked up. She looked down at him; blood dripped down from the open wound on the back of her head. She squeezed his face, digging her nails into his cheeks.

'You killed me, you killed me,' his wife Barbara screamed into his face every night, until his final breath.

# CHAPTER SIXTY-THREE
# THE WRITER

The butterfly has its moment in the sun, but for every summer a winter follows, and the creature will not see the following summer.

You will never be a butterfly – never.

All these years I have written you these silly little letters giving you hope, the hope that there is an eternal life waiting for you. That the ridiculous books you have written (don't forget you wrote the Book of Truth and the scriptures) are somehow true. You are not a god.

Let me tell you a secret: you will never be forgiven for all your sins; if there is a hell you will burn.

As she had done many times before, she pressed down and wax sealed the envelope, but this time she didn't post the letter to his house – she didn't post it at all. She put Harold's name and the prison address on the envelope, but she'd had second thoughts about sending the letter. She wasn't sure but she believed that in all prisons the post would be vetted, and she wasn't sure this kind of post would be allowed. Was it threatening? She wasn't sure, but she hoped it was.

# CHAPTER SIXTY-FOUR
# HAROLD AND THE WRITER

This would be her first and last visit to see Harold in prison. She had been given a morning slot but had to arrive ten minutes early to sign some papers and check she had nothing dangerous or expensive on her person; she was then scanned and patted down. She could see him seated and waiting. He was so much older than she remembered and a lot gaunter than the pictures she'd seen in the newspapers lately. She slowly walked over and sat opposite him.

'Hello, stranger,' Harold said, and winked.

She said nothing for a while and just took in the scene. There were some other prisoners sitting and chatting to their visitors, probably friends or family; she was neither of these to Harold. She thought the other prisoners sitting nearby looked far more dangerous than Harold, some with tattoos and skinheads and others just looking plain scary, and she didn't dare look their way for too long. Others looked timid, but that's the thing – looks can be deceiving; this was where Harold belonged.

For many years she'd thought of all the things she wanted to say to him, but now she sat opposite him for the first time since he'd tried to kill her, she was lost for words.

'You know my mum is dead,' Tiff said.

'Yes, I do,' Harold said, and nodded.

'Good riddance is what I say,' Tiff said. 'She was evil, like you.'

'I would expect you to think like that,' Harold said. 'The main problem she had was she let you go. The Utal ...' Tiff cut him off.

'The eternal life that the Utal offers, the forgiveness,' Tiff said. 'Surely she should have realised.'

'Yes, you are understanding now,' Harold said.

'No, do you not understand sarcasm?' Tiff said. 'What she should have realised was you are crazy,' Tiff said. 'All those years ago you ruined her life with the drivel you spouted to her and she was stupid enough or evil enough to go along with you.'

'Your mum was weak and so are you,' Harold said. 'I think we're done here, unless you have a reason for your visit – do you?'

Tiff waited a brief moment and put her hand out for Harold to be quiet.

'The butterfly flitters and glides, exuberant colours and pollen fill its senses and dark red petals reflect against its symmetrical wings,' Tiff said. 'Through its spiracles, oxygen pulsates through its body. Life is beautiful, with not a care in the world.'

'No. How have you seen the Utal's letters to me?' Harold asked.

Tiff ignored him and continued.

'Life hasn't always been this way,' Tiff said. 'The end was the beginning as the words he'd longed to hear resonated through his mind. He was cleansed and all of his faults and sins faded and kept doing so until they were completely diluted and disappeared. And his life began.'

'You stole my letters,' Harold said. 'That is the only possible reason you would know about these letters, about the butterfly.'

'No, Harold, I wrote them. I wanted revenge for me and for your wife Barbara,' Tiff said. 'You see, you tried to kill me and your poor wife saved me and she got slaughtered for it.'

'The Utal offers forgiveness. I have done what he asked; I'm a hero – you should be thanking me,' Harold said, raising his voice.

Tiff laughed.

'Careful, Harold,' Tiff said. 'You might be taken back to your cell early and I'm not done here.'

'We are done. Everything you say is a lie,' Harold said.

'It is the truth and the truth can be hard to take,' Tiff said. 'And you need to understand that there is no forgiveness for what you've done.'

'Lies – only the Utal can give me forgiveness,' Harold said. 'You wouldn't be able to comprehend this, I know.'

'Now, this is very important,' Tiff said. 'I want to make myself perfectly clear. I know you'll deny this fact and that's because there is something not quite right in your head, but I will make this as easy for you to understand as possible. You wrote your silly Book of Truth and the scriptures. You were not chosen and there are no believers or constants. I wrote the letters to you. I knew you'd try something stupid and this time I was making sure you went to prison for it.'

Harold's mood changed and he smiled.

'Then you committed murder – you helped kill Jay,' Harold said.

'No, that's not what happened – that's not what I said,' Tiff said. 'You see, I tracked down your grandchild Lewis, the one you refuse to admit is your grandchild. It was easy to get him onside and that's because he hates you as much as I do. He was supposed to make sure you attacked him or Jay, but that you didn't harm anyone. There were two of them and you are feeble, frail – you would have been easy to stop.'

'But that's not what happened, is it? Harold said.

'Well, no. I didn't know Lewis had your crazy genes, did I now?' Tiff said.

'You were there on the night, weren't you?' Harold asked her.

Tiff didn't say anything.

'You screamed – it was you. I heard somebody scream. I told Lewis, but he told me I was crazy and I was hearing things,' Harold said. 'But he must have known you were there. That's it, isn't it? You came to see me die and I didn't,' Harold laughed.

Tiff still didn't say anything; she couldn't. She didn't know what to say – it was true.

'You can sit and pretend but we both know Jay would still be alive if it weren't for your supposed letters,' Harold said. 'And if you claim to have written them, then you are as guilty as me.'

Tears rolled down Tiff's cheeks and she got up from her seat, looked at Harold for one last time and left.

'In the Utal we trust,' Harold whispered, as he stared at Tiff's back until she'd left the visitors' room.

# CHAPTER SIXTY-FIVE
## LEWIS
## A COUPLE OF MONTHS AFTER HAROLD WENT TO JAIL

'It's time we drew a line under this and moved on,' Lewis'
mum, Jane, said. 'Would you agree with me, Lewis?' She put
her hand on his shoulder.

'Agreed. Thanks, Mum. So you're not going to visit him
again, are you?' Lewis said. 'That is moving on, together.'

'He is in prison and has no other living family. I don't
think it's right …' his mum started to say.

'But I should forget about my grandad. One rule for you
and one me – am I hearing you correctly?' Lewis asked.

'No, he's my dad if you like it or not,' his mum said. 'And
he's your grandad too, but I don't need him to tell me he's
my dad; I don't need him to tell me he loves me. Me and him
spending time together is enough. You, on the other hand
…'

'You know he was trying to kill Jay. You do know that,
right? You know I was arrested because of him?' Lewis
asked.

'We've been through this with him and his lawyers – he has taken the blame for you,' his mum said. 'You don't need to carry on with this act.'

'It would be nice if you believed me for once, Mum,' Lewis said. 'I did it – I've told you I hit Jay but I didn't mean to kill him. Harold planned to use him as a sacrifice for his stupid Book of Truth, this is the difference, like he did to his wife. I've had enough of you,' Lewis said, and stormed off.

Later in the evening, Lewis sat on his bed, bouncing his tennis ball on the ceiling with the soul intention to annoy his mum. He was waiting to hear his mum shout up the stairs at him, but then heard a rumbling sound and his bed started to rock. He got off it, crouched down on to his hands and knees, and looked underneath his bed. Something shot out towards him. Lewis screwed up his eyes and braced himself, then nothing – all went quiet. He looked down and he saw it lying in front of him – it was looking up at him; he couldn't believe it.

'The Book of Truth,' Lewis said, and he picked up the dusty old book, the book he'd burnt, the book he'd watch turn into nothing but ashes, ashes he'd seen vanish into the night.

'Don't be afraid. Don't listen to your grandad. Why don't you read the next chapter?' Lewis heard a weird voice say to him.

The End.